BREAKING UP WITH MY BOSS

LOVE YOU FOREVER-BOOK 4

ALEXIS WINTER

OKAY, SO TAKING A GOLF CLUB TO
MY BOSS'S PRECIOUS SPORTS CAR
WAS PROBABLY AN OVERREACTION—
BUT DAMN DID IT FEEL GOOD.

**However, him showing up at my house to blackmail me
into marrying him…WTF?**

If there's one person that can make me hate my very existence,
It's Matthew Lewis III, my boss from hell.
Imagine the devil's younger, sexy brother in a three-piece suit.

He's the kind of man that makes any sort of rational thought go right
out the window—which is exactly where I want to throw him.

So when he ripped me a new one for being TWO minutes late,
I lost my shit.
I not only gave him a piece of my mind, but I also ripped his prissy ass
to shreds and marched out with my middle fingers in the air.
I'd rather be homeless on the streets of Chicago than work for
that man.

But my victory was short-lived.
Here I am face to face with an ultimatum…

I either face a felony or pretend for a few short months that I love him.

GAME ON.

I just hope he's ready to give me an f-ing Oscar for this performance. But after meeting his grandma, I find out Matthew has one giant secret he doesn't want me to know,
And I have to face the fact that maybe...just maybe, my performance isn't so fake after all.

You know how they say there's a thin line between love and hate? I think that line might have just disappeared.

ONE

POPPY

My alarm clock goes off at 6 a.m. on the dot, but I smack the snooze button and let out an overly dramatic groan. I'm not much of a morning person. In fact, I loathe mornings and everything that goes with them: breakfast, coffee, newspapers, and cheery morning people. The thought of any of it makes me want to cry and hide under my blankets till noon rolls around.

As I drift in and out of sleep, I think about what my day will bring. Probably the usual: my boss reprimanding me for my *bad attitude*, being chastised for rolling my eyes, and jumping to fulfill every ridiculous fucking demand that rolls into his thick head. If I don't get my ass out of this bed, I'll also end up rushing to get ready—probably getting to work late and once again getting bitched out by my boss who I hate almost as much as I hate mornings.

Of all the people in this world, I had to end up working for Matthew Lewis III, also known as Satan's younger, hotter brother. He's good-looking and he knows it, which is the worst—cocky, arrogant, and rich as hell. With a name like that, of course he is. Honestly, I have no idea why he's even working as a lawyer at the firm. He told Daniel it had more to do with an honest day's work, being fulfilled, and getting out from under his overbearing father's thumb. I personally think it's all a crock of shit. I just know the devil put him here to torture me any way he could. Why would I be on the devil's radar you ask? I have no idea, but I think I did something in my past life that I'm still being punished for today. That's my best guess, anyway.

The alarm goes off again, and this time, I shut the damn thing off and sit up with a groan. "Why does my life suck?" I ask looking up toward the ceiling as if God is listening to me. I put my feet on the floor and raise my steepled hands. "I swear, I'll be a better person. I'll live a better life. Just get me out of this shit job . . . and winning the lottery wouldn't hurt. Just saying," I add on to whomever or whatever is listening.

I trudge my way to the shower and step beneath the hot flow of water, letting it rain down over my head to wash my hair and body. After I'm done, I feel like I have some extra time since I didn't over-sleep too much today, so I sit on the shower floor, letting the water warm me from the outside in. Pretty soon, I'm warm, comfy, and falling back asleep. The next thing I know, cold water is waking me like I've been shocked. I have no idea how long I've been sitting there, but by the looks of my pruny fingers, it's been a touch too long. I jump up and turn off the water, wrapping myself in a towel as I make my way to the bedroom to get dressed.

My teeth are chattering so much that I feel like I'm in a *Scooby-Doo* episode. I'm too cold to move, so I climb back into bed and pull the blankets around me. "Mmm, that's better," I mumble to myself as my eyes close. I open them quickly to check the time. 7 a.m.

Shit! I passed out for another 30 minutes. I throw off the blanket and push my numb toes out of mind as I dress as quickly as possible. I don't have time to blow-dry or do much with my hair, so I gather the long auburn locks into my hand and wrap them around to form a bun, pinning it down. I throw on some mascara and lip gloss and call it a good job.

I'm walking into the office and I'm literally only two minutes late, but does that matter to Mr. Matthew Lewis III? Ha, no. Late is late,

and he's already standing at my desk with a slip. Who even uses phys-
ical slips in this day and age?

I want to stop dead in my tracks when I see him, but I push
myself forward anyway. He holds out the slip and I take it as I pass.

"Third day in a row, Ms. Russell." He begins *tsk-tsk*ing me.

"I'm sorry, Mr. Lewis, but—" I start with my excuses.

"What? What is it today? Did your bus crash and go up in
flames? Let me guess . . . you rescued 20 homeless children from a fire
and when the media arrived, you tried to sneak off because you didn't
want the fame, but they forced you into the limelight and now you
have to lose the press who are hot on your trail? Something like that,
right?"

I cock my head to the side, face void of all amusement. "No, my
cat is sick and puked in my lap while I was having breakfast. I had to
change. I couldn't come in here smelling like cat vomit."

He shakes his head. "It's always something with you. When will
you come out with the truth and tell me you're a complete failure at
time management? One more slip-up from you and I'm afraid I'll
have to let you go." He takes off, back to his office.

Daniel exits his office and smirks in my direction. "You have to
admit, you're not very good at getting here on time."

I scoff. "I'm not good at getting *anywhere* on time. At this point,
I'm fairly certain I'll be late for my own funeral."

He laughs but continues on his way to the copy room.

I try to focus all my attention on the task at hand: logging in to my
computer, turning on my phone, and checking my email for the daily
list of appointments and tasks.

The intercom on my desk buzzes. "Poppy, do you have my first
client's file ready?"

I roll my eyes. How am I supposed to have their file ready when I
haven't even seen who the first client is yet? I press the button and
reply in my sweet voice. "I'm doing it now."

He's right back with, "How many times have I told you to get the
files pulled the day before?"

Ugh. I know, I know. It makes sense to do it that way, and it would result in a much easier start to the day, but I'm always so busy in the afternoon that I forget or simply don't have time. And if I'm honest, by the time 5 p.m. rolls around, it's all I can do to get the hell out of this office before I snap at Mr. Lewis.

"I'm pulling the file now, sir," I say through gritted teeth, ignoring his question.

The computer finally loads and I'm able to pull up the appointment book to see who our first client of the day is: *Anderson, Samuel.* I rush to the filing cabinet behind me and pull the file, taking it into his office. "Here you go. Sam Anderson's file. He should be here in 10 minutes." I'm feeling proud of myself for doing that so quickly. On another note, why the hell does he insist on using paper files when he has access to the e-files? Just another Matthew-ism that makes me want to staple this damn file to his forehead.

"Thank you," he says, taking the file from my hand. "Did you remember to start your phone up? We can't book clients if the phone isn't working, and if we can't book clients, we're both out of a job. Surely I don't have to explain that to you." He runs a hand across his smooth, angular jaw as his lips turn up into a smirk.

"I understand how it works," I say, spinning around to switch on my phone before he calls it and finds out I haven't done it yet. As soon as I'm out of his sight, I sprint to my desk, nearly diving for my phone. I tap in my code and the phone resets. It's on.

"I'm going to guess that your lack of answer means you haven't done it yet," he says from his office.

"What are you talking about? It's on. See?" I pick it up and press the first button to call his phone.

It rings and he answers with, "Good timing." Then he hangs up.

I collapse into my desk chair and let out a long sigh. Fuck. Today sucks already. After taking a moment to catch my breath, I pull up the schedule and pull the files for every client we have coming in today. I stack them on the corner of my desk. That way, each client who comes in already has a file ready, so I can grab it on the way to Mr. Lewis' office.

Once that task is finished, I look at my email to see the things I've received overnight. This is usually just a long, stupid list of things my boss would like me to do, such as: *Call Mr. Easton to follow up on his last appointment, confirm that he's happy, and ensure he doesn't have any further questions. Book appointment if necessary.*

By lunch, I've made all the calls and whittled down my list to just a few things. I knock on Mr. Lewis' door. "Lunch call," I say, opening it up to find him sitting at his desk.

He doesn't pull his attention away from his work. He just holds up a slip of paper that contains his lunch order even though it's the same damn thing every damn day. I walk over, take the paper, and turn around to leave, saying, "It's always a pleasure, Mr. Lewis." I let the door close a little too loudly behind me.

I swing by the sandwich shop and get his usual turkey breast on rye with lettuce, mayo, and mustard. After paying for his order, I grab myself a shake-and-go salad from the cooler at checkout and head back to the office to have lunch at my desk. After giving Mr. Ungrateful his sandwich, I go back to my desk to eat. I pour my fat-free salad dressing on the salad, replace the lid, and shake it up. I've only had one bite when he's calling me back to his office. With a sigh, I stand up and walk in there.

He has his sandwich open and lying on his desk. "What is this shit?" he asks, motioning toward it.

I take a few steps in, peering at the sandwich. "It looks like turkey breast on rye with lettuce, mayo, and mustard."

He glares at me. "This is low-fat mayo; it tastes like saddle soap." Of course little rich boy knows what saddle soap tastes like.

"Horse lessons as a child?" I ask, trying to hide my judgment.

"What?" he replies, confused and clearly not picking up on my sarcasm.

I shake my head but pick up the sandwich and toss it into the bag.

"Would you like me to get you something else?" I ask before walking out of his office.

"No, I've lost my appetite. It's the same damn lunch every single day, Poppy. I swear, if you're not screwing something up, you're not doing it at all."

I can't take the smug, arrogant look on his face any longer. "Oh, screw you, Matthew Lewis III! What kind of fucking name is that anyway? Who were you named after—Thurston Howell from *Gilligan's Island*?"

He looks up at me like I've lost my mind, but maybe I have. Maybe I'm tired of putting up with his prissy ass. What man worries about the mayo on his damn sandwich? I guess the same kind that requires non-dairy, low-fat French vanilla creamer for his coffee every morning.

"What did you say to me?" he asks slowly and quietly, like he can't believe I've insulted him in such a disrespectful manner.

"Which part? The part about your ridiculous name or the part about you being named after a character from *Gilligan's Island*? I can't keep track with you anymore."

"That's it. That's the last straw," he says, sitting down and opening his desk drawer for what I can only assume is a termination slip. "I'm sick of you always being late." His hand scribbles across the slip. "I'm tired of the stupid-ass excuses." He looks up at me. "I mean, come on, a grade school kid has more believable excuses than you." He goes back to writing. "And I'm tired of you either not doing something or screwing it up when you do. You're fired." He says, tearing off the slip and trying to hand it over.

My eyes widen and my mouth falls open. "I'm fired? I'm *fired*?" I yell, taking the bag with his sandwich in it and throwing it onto his lap. "Good fucking riddance, you entitled prick! You think you're going to keep an assistant with your attitude? With your whiny *I'm rich and better than you* demeanor? Ha! Good fucking luck. Deuces, Mr. Matthew Lewis III, Esquire." I throw both middle fingers in the air and leave his office, slamming the door behind me. Daniel has clearly overheard everything and he's leaning against my desk with his arms crossed over his chest, laughing his ass off.

"What's so funny?" I ask, moving around my desk and grabbing my things. Lucky for me, I don't have much here—just my purse, jacket, and phone.

He shakes his head. "I've just never heard anyone tell him off like that before. Funny shit."

"Well, I'm sorry your entertainment for the day is leaving, but as I'm sure you just heard, I've been fired."

He waves his hand through the air. "I'm sure you'll be back." He stands up to walk to his office.

"Don't hold your breath," I say just as the door clicks shut.

I spin on my heel and head for the exit, more than ready to put this place behind me. As I'm about to push through the door, Matthew's golf clubs catch my attention. That asshole deserves everything that's coming to him. Maybe I should help karma out a little. I grab a club and take it out with me. In the garage where he parks—because his priceless sports car is worth far too much money to leave in the parking lot with us common folk—I lift the golf club and swing, smashing out a headlight. It feels so good to let the aggression out. My body floods with endorphins and powers me to do more. I move to the other side and swing again, busting out the other headlight. I move around the car, swinging at the taillights. I'm tired and my breathing is heavy.

I'm about to drop the club and walk away when I think of one last thing. I climb up on the hood and swing again and again, busting the windshield. I'm sure I look like a crazed lunatic, but I don't care—destroying something he loves is pure elation.

"Hey! Stop!" someone yells. I toss the club, grab my purse off the ground, and take off running.

TWO

MATTHEW

Daniel walks into my office with a smirk on his face.

"Don't start with me, man." I lift my hand and massage my temples.

He laughs as he sits down in the chair across from my desk. "You need to give it up. We both know why you're so hard on her."

"Because she's incompetent," I say matter-of-factly.

He shakes his head. "It's because you have a thing for her. It's okay. Just admit it."

I feel my eyes stretch wide. "Have a thing for her? *Her?*" I point toward the door.

He nods, smile still in place.

"Not in million years, my friend. Have you seen the women I've had on my arm? I could have 12 just like her—better than her, even." I know I sound like a complete dick, but goddamn if she doesn't bring it out of me.

"No," he says, still shaking his head. "She's the only one you can't have—the only one who stands up to you and tells you exactly what she thinks whether you like it or not, and that drives you crazy."

I open my mouth to argue, but my phone rings and I stop to answer it. "Hello?"

"Sorry to bother you, Mr. Lewis, but this is Jeff from security in the parking garage. You're not going to be happy, but there was just a woman in here beating the ever-loving shit out of your car with a golf club. We have it on video if you'd like to press charges. Should I call the police?"

"Not yet. I'll be right over." I hang up the phone and shoot Daniel a look.

"What was that about?" he asks, standing up and watching me round my desk.

"She beat the shit out of my car with my own fucking golf club," I say, heading for the door. All I hear behind me is Daniel's loud laughter.

I get to the parking garage and go straight to my car. I nearly fall to my knees when I see the busted windshield, headlights, and tail-lights. "Oh, what did she do to you?" I ask my car, reaching out to rub my hand across her hood. This Audi R8 isn't just a luxury supercar . . . this is my baby.

"We're really sorry, Mr. Lewis. We tried getting here in time, but the damage was already done and she took off running. Would you like to watch the footage?"

I'm speechless but I nod.

"Right this way."

He leads me to the security room and pulls up the footage. I watch the black-and-white screen as she comes into view, holding my golf club. She drops her purse on the ground and takes the club in both hands. It sails through the air, smashing against the first head-light, causing me to flinch. She works her way around the car and looks to be done, but then at the last minute, she climbs up onto the hood and swings again and again until the windshield is completely shattered. Her head whips around quickly, apparently getting caught in the act, then she jumps down, tosses the golf club, and takes off running—grabbing her purse as she passes it.

"Would you like for us to call the police, sir?"

"No," I answer. "I'm going to handle this privately. But will you send me this footage?"

"Sure thing, boss."

As I'm leaving, I pull out my phone and call a tow truck to take the car away. I call the garage ahead of time to let them know my car is coming in, and I don't hang up until they promise to make her beautiful again. Then I go back to my office to think about what it is I want to do.

Daniel wasn't wrong. I've had a thing for Poppy since the day she walked into my office in that short skirt with red fuck-me pumps, which were completely inappropriate for a professional setting. Those shoes, though, were sexy as fuck, and they gave her long, tan legs a nice shape—a shape I thought I'd for sure see wrapped around my hips. But that hasn't happened, and that's because from the moment I hired her, she's hated me.

I have high expectations for all of my employees. If I hire you for a job, I want the job completed on time and my way. Poppy and I have butted heads too many times. She's constantly tardy, she's never prepared, and she's always a mess. She can't keep things tidy while working. She has a one-task-at-a-time mindset, and I can't stand those kinds of people. Hasn't anyone heard of multitasking? I do it every damn day. It's not that hard. Why didn't I fire her immediately? I don't have a fucking clue. I guess I thought I could train her, and self-ishly, I was probably thinking with my dick.

I could easily press charges against her now, but where would that get me? She doesn't have the kind of money it'll take to fix my car. She could be thrown in jail, but that doesn't get me anything either. I still have to deal with the damage she's caused. There's only one way out of this that will get me exactly what I want.

After my last client leaves at the end of the day, I grab my things and head out to the parking lot where the dealership delivered my rental. I get behind the wheel and drive over to her place. It's an apartment building in Lincoln Park. The area is trendy, but the building seems pre-war and a little run-down. I see her name next to a buzzer but notice the door isn't even latched, so anyone off the street could just walk into the building. This is completely unacceptable for anyone—let alone her.

I take the stairs up to the third floor and knock on her door. The door opens but the chain is still in place. At least she's smart when it comes to safety, but that little chain isn't going to stop someone who really wants to get in. I see shock register on her face before disdain quickly replaces it.

"What are you doing here?" she asks through the cracked door.

"I came to talk to you," I reply, trying to keep my tone light.

"Talk to me? I think we've done enough of that. You can go to hell." She tries closing the door, but I put my foot in the way, preventing it from shutting.

"I think you're going to want to hear me out."

She flashes me an annoyed smile. "And why would I do something stupid like that?"

"Simple." I pull out my phone and flip the screen around to show her the footage of her smashing the shit out of my car.

Her eyes move from my face down to the phone.

"If you don't, I'll press charges."

She takes a deep breath and clenches her teeth. I can tell by the way her jaw is flexing that she's realizing she's screwed.

"Fine."

I remove my foot and she shuts the door. I hear the chain sliding across it and then the door is back open.

I step inside and follow her down a short hallway and into the living room, where she sits on the couch. I look around the room. "This place isn't very safe," I tell her.

Her mouth drops open. "Thanks, Mr. Lewis, I appreciate your concern for my safety, but I'm fine."

"Hey, I'm not here for the pleasantries." I take a seat in the chair that's facing her.

"What are you here for anyway?"

"Simple. I need you and you need me."

She scrunches up her nose. "Why do I need you?"

"Well, you need a job, don't you? How else are you going to afford all this?" I gesture facetiously around the apartment.

She rolls her eyes. "And why do you need me?"

"Ah, see, that's a little more complicated." I sit up, resting my elbows on my knees as I keep my eyes on her. "You see, I've had this problem for some time now. My grandmother, who means the world to me, is very sick and dying."

"Oh no," she breathes out, already feeling sorry for me, the poor little rich boy.

"She's very special to me because after my mother passed away, she was all I had. My father was too busy working, and if it hadn't been for my grandmother, I would've been raised by whomever my dad could hire."

She nods, understanding.

"Her one wish in all the world is to see me married."

Her eyes go wide. "I AM NOT marrying you."

I snort. "Don't be stupid. I'm not asking you to marry me. I'm asking you to pretend to be my fiancée for a little while—just until she passes."

She takes a deep breath and lets it out slowly. Then she stands up and starts pacing. "How long does she have to live?"

"The doctors have given her six to nine months, but we don't think she'll make it that long. Her quality of life is diminishing every day."

"And how often would we have to put this show on? Like, once a month or something at family functions?"

"I have dinner with my grandmother every Friday night, and then there's family brunch every Sunday."

"Twice a week?" she asks, her voice rising and her eyes widening.

"For starters. There will be events here and there that I'll have to attend for family obligations. Business deals, mergers, that sort of thing. But this isn't an *I rarely call on you here and there* kind of thing.

If you accept, this will be a *day in and day out* kind of deal. We have to sell it, which means we'll have to get to know each other on a personal level. Not anything like how we are now."

"Ugh," she groans, falling back into her seat on the couch. "So not only do I have to come back to work for you where I'll see you all day, but I also have to get to know you all night?"

"That's right," I agree with a nod and a smile.

She shakes her head. "Nope, no way."

"All right. I guess I'll just go ahead and call the police and turn in this video. You know that's a felony, right?" I ask, pulling out my phone. "Get that pretty face ready for your mug shot, sweetheart."

"Wait." Her head falls back, causing her silky hair to fall off her shoulders. Her eyes close like she's praying to the gods. "I'll do it. I'll come back to work for you and I'll play this stupid little game."

"Good. Thought you'd see it my way. First things first: pack your shit."

Her head pops up. "What? Pack?"

"Yeah, my fiancée can't live in a shit place like this. You'll be moving in with me for the time being. My rental is downstairs. Bring what you can for now and we'll have movers get the rest later. I'll see you down there," I say with a smile as I head for the door. I put my hand on the knob but freeze. "No cats allowed at my place."

She frowns. "I don't have a cat."

All those fucking cat excuses and she doesn't even have a cat? Yep, I'm feeling a lot better about my decision. I'm going to make her pay.

THREE

POPPY

How the hell do I get myself into these messes? What have I done? I was happy to be rid of that job and him, and now I'm moving in with the guy? How is this normal? Do fake fiancée contracts actually exist, or am I trapped in some weird alternate universe?

I'm muttering a long string of cuss words as I'm shoving shit into my bag. If he's going to make me do this, then I'm going to make it way more difficult than it has to be. He thinks I'm a pain in the ass? He hasn't seen nothing yet! I grab every bag I own and fill them with random shit—even shit I don't wear or haven't worn in years. I pack every pair of shoes I have and every random product in my bathroom. I take the first load down: six bags that nearly take me to the ground, but I manage. I stop in front of the car he's leaning against. It's another ostentatious two-seater sports car. Go figure. Makes me wonder if he's trying to make up for his lack of a personality . . . or maybe even a micropenis. I smirk to myself imagining that God cursed him with a teeny weenie as a way to keep him humble with his East Coast money and frat-boy good looks.

"Here's half of it," I say, dropping the stuff on the concrete and turning around to get the rest.

"What the fuck is this?"

"My stuff. You wanted me to move in with you, yes?" I pause. "I'm going to need clothes if you don't want me walking around your house naked." I continue on, getting the rest of the stuff I packed.

By the grace of God, we manage to squeeze into the car that's loaded down from top to bottom with my bags. I have bags under my feet that keep my knees in my chest. I have bags on my lap so high that I can't even see where we're going. There are bags stuffed into the trunk and up between us. I can't see a thing from behind all of my belongings, but I have a feeling it's for the best, because it feels like he's driving like a bat out of hell.

He jerks the wheel and makes a fast, sharp turn that has the tires squealing off the pavement. One of the bags between us falls into his lap.

"What *is* this shit?" he asks, grabbing the bag and tossing it out the window.

"Hey!" I yell, trying to turn back to see which bag it was so I can remember what was in it.

"Trust me, whatever was in there isn't worth the hassle. I'll replace whatever's gone," he promises, and knowing his taste, it dawns on me that the items that come up missing will have brand-new designer replacements. I smile as I start to think that maybe this isn't such a bad deal after all.

"You ever heard of littering, asshole?" I say, gripping the bag on my lap for dear life.

We get to his place and I'm surprised to find he lives in a penthouse suite. The building is nicer than anything I've ever been in, but for some reason, I was expecting some Bruce Wayne mansion hidden away behind impenetrable brick walls. We each grab several bags and silently make our way to the elevator. I notice he doesn't push a button but instead scans a key fob as the elevator smoothly makes its way to the top floor.

When the doors open to the grand foyer, he steps inside and leads me through the living room and down the hall to a bedroom. "This will be your room. You have a bathroom through there," he points at a door. "And that's the closet." He points at another door. "Dinner is prepared and on the table by 7 p.m. nightly, and you are to attend. That's when we'll get to know each other." He turns and heads for the door. "See you in an hour. I suggest you unpack and get cleaned up." The door closes a little too loudly, sealing my fate as I live out the rest of my miserable life.

As doomed as things seem, I can't help but feel a tiny bit excited with this predicament. No sense in treating this as a punishment. I have a bedroom the size of my apartment, and a luxury marble bathroom full of bubbles and oils. I'm going to enjoy every minute of making his life miserable. I smile as I throw myself back on the bed. It's thick and soft and hugs my body like it was made for me.

I unpack some things—leaving most of it in bags because it's stuff I never use, then I freshen up for dinner. I leave my room at 7:02 p.m., just because I know it will drive him crazy. As expected, he's already at the table with restaurant-quality place settings. I take my seat and place a cloth napkin on my lap.

"I specifically said dinner is at 7 p.m. on the dot. It's two minutes past. How the hell can you be late when you don't even have to go anywhere?" he nearly yells.

I shrug and offer a smirk. "Real talent," I say, only pissing him off more.

He flexes his jaw and I can tell he's doing everything he can to hold back his anger, but instead of saying anything, he just starts making his plate and handing the serving dishes off to me.

I fill my plate with a fresh salad, pasta, and garlic bread, then he pours us each a glass of wine. I can't help but look around the dining room as we eat. The table we're sitting at is long and made of a thick, dark wood. I bet we could easily fit 20 people around it. On the far wall is an expensive-looking cabinet filled with fine china and drinkware—crystal, no doubt. There's more money in this room than I've spent in my whole life. I'm sure of it.

"So, tell me about yourself, Poppy," he says in his deep voice that always makes my heart thrum.

I take a deep breath and wipe my mouth with the cloth napkin. "What would you like to know?"

"Let's start with our pasts, shall we?"

"Okay," I agree, allowing my eyes to drink him in—from the top of his neatly combed dark hair to his even darker eyes and sharp, angular jaw. Fuck, if he could just keep his mouth shut, I could easily find myself attracted to him beyond just acknowledging his good looks. Too bad that's ruined the moment he talks. "Well, I was raised in the country. My father worked at a lumber yard and my mother was a grade-school teacher."

"Ha!" he scoffs.

"What?" I immediately feel my back stiffen.

He's chewing and shaking his head. "You were raised by a teacher, yet 90 percent of the memos you craft for me have spelling and grammatical errors. Ironic."

Are you fucking kidding me? Who says this shit? What an ass. But that's okay; he'll pay for it soon enough. "I said GRADE SCHOOL. It's not like she taught the kids college English. Anyway, as I was saying before I was so rudely interrupted, I grew up in the country and it was fun. I had a good childhood even though my parents didn't make a lot of money. I never knew the difference until I was a teenager anyway, and by then, I'd already learned that if you wanted something in life, you had to work for it."

"Well, I'm glad to see that while your parents couldn't afford the nicer things, they still instilled good values in you."

I roll my eyes. "Yeah, believe it or not, I wasn't raised by a pack of wolves." I find my left hand balled into a fist under the table with my nails digging into my palm.

"Of course you weren't. You have a basic understanding of modern technology considering how much time you spend on your cell phone. I wouldn't expect that from a real-life Mowgli. Please, continue," he says, urging me on with a wave of his hand. Classic Matthew Lewis—never letting a fucking verbal jab go unsaid.

"I made good grades in school and was in honors classes. I would've been valedictorian, but I got beat out by Stella Harris because I got mono my senior year and missed a week."

"Mono, huh? I had that once too. They call it the kissing disease, you know."

I draw my brows together. "What's that supposed to mean?"

"I mean, were you a *never been kissed* type of girl or were you a *girls gone wild* type?"

I scoff. "What does that have to do with anything?" I'm trying really hard to not be offended, but it's a hard feat at this point. It's like he's trying to piss me off. That's when I realize that's exactly what he's trying to do. He's trying to piss me off. And I'm not giving him the satisfaction.

He shrugs. "Just want to know what I'm getting into. That's all."

"I don't have a boyfriend now, if that's what you're asking. And you're not *getting into* this," I say dramatically with air quotes.

He chews the food in his mouth and swallows. "That's part of it, but also, are you a random hookup type of girl? Am I going to have to worry about introducing you to people only to realize you've already screwed them?"

Fuck this asshole! "No, I'm not a random hookup type of girl. I think you'll be safe."

"I'm just trying to cover the bases here; no need to take it personally."

My back straightens. "You know what? Why don't you tell me about yourself?" This way, I can throw insults his way.

"All right," he agrees, putting his fork down and wiping his mouth. "I was raised here and at our second home in Malibu. My father, as you know, works with the stock market. Many years later, he ventured out into—"

"Excuse me, but I asked you to tell me about *you*. Not your father."

He swallows and I see his left eye twitch—one of the tells that he's close to biting my head off. "Very well," he grinds the words out between clenched teeth. "I went to a private prep school where I dominated in academics and sports. I was at the top of my class even though I got mono. And I graduated with honors. From there I went to Harvard, and then to Harvard Law School. The plan was to become a lawyer so I could be hired on at my father's company, but I was so sick of him and his life that I shunned his offer and ventured out on my own."

"And by going out on your own, you mean you took your trust fund and started the life you have now, right?" I say motioning around the room with my fork.

He nods slowly. "I did have a trust fund," he reluctantly agrees.

"So all that talk about working for what you want in life was just bullshit?"

His back straightens. "No! I do work for what I want in life."

"You do *now*, but you had a nice, cushy bank account to get you started."

"Your point?"

"My point is, how do you think you'd be living right now if you hadn't inherited that trust fund? Would you be living like me in a shitty apartment—wearing clothes you bought from the thrift shop? I mean, you'd be buried in student loan debt. And I bet Harvard would set you back a lot more than my four-year state school—that is, if you could've even gotten in without your father's connections."

"All right, yes, I will admit that there may be some privilege, but I do work for everything I have now."

"I'm just saying that the people you think are below you are just the same as you, but they didn't have a head start in life. They started from the bottom—not already on top."

"Clearly, we're not playing nice tonight," he breathes out, picking up his wine glass.

"I'm sorry, I didn't get the memo. I just assumed by the shots you were firing my way that it went both ways."

He pushes away from the table. "I'll speak with you tomorrow, Poppy. Try to not be late in the morning. You'll be riding with me and I leave at 6:30 a.m. sharp." He leaves the dining room and I finally feel comfortable enough to eat.

FOUR

MATTHEW

I swear, nothing can aggravate me as much as that woman in there can. Would it kill her to show a little respect? I suppose I was a little hard on her when she was speaking, because I was searching for any way to piss her off. I have to give it to her . . . she did manage to hold her tongue pretty well. Those are exactly the tools she'll need when she meets my father. I might as well prepare her for what lies ahead.

After getting pissed off at dinner, I go straight to my bathroom to take a steam in my custom sauna before showering. I don't know what the hell it is about Poppy Russell that drives me wild while simultaneously bringing out the worst in me. I hate that Daniel is right: I treat her like shit because I'm an asshole—an asshole who can't get her out of my mind. The way she always chews her bottom lip when she's scrambling to meet my demands, the way she always looks like she half-rolled out of bed . . . something about it just makes me want to bend her over my knee before stripping her naked and worshipping her lithe body.

I'd love to know how she maintains her perfect physique—that tiny waist and those long, lean legs. I lean my head back against the wall as I replay the way she bent over my desk last week. She was frantically mopping up the cup of coffee she'd just spilled on my desk, and instead of being pissed, I couldn't get past how close her bare neck was to my lips. I inhaled her floral scent and had to physically restrain myself from slipping a hand behind her head and kissing her full, pouty lips. She almost caught me too. She turned around and the look on her face reminded me that I should be angry, so I quickly jumped up and shouted at her. I hate that I've played this role for so long that she thinks I actually hate her. I'd give anything to start over, grow some balls, and ask her out. Now she's my fake fiancée and I need to figure out a way to really sell it.

Which reminds me: I need to get her a ring. And unfortunately, it has to be a real one. One look from my father or grandmother and they'll know it's fake and that this whole thing is a sham. But can I even trust her forgetful ass with a $20,000 diamond? Probably not. She'd probably lose it and say that her nonexistent cat ate it. Then she'd turn around and ask me for money to pay for its pretend surgery to retrieve it. No doubt, the vet from Joke's-on-You clinic wouldn't be able to recover it, and I'd have an imaginary cat worth $20,000.

While I steam, I keep coming up with ways to torture her. She definitely needs some fine-tuning if I expect her to pass my father and grandmother's harsh judgments. If she thinks I'm judgmental, she hasn't seen anything yet. I guess I could spoil her with a spa day so she'll be more apt to listen to my other suggestions. Maybe that'll help soften the blow when I tell her she needs a few etiquette lessons. She needs to know when to use the small fork and how to butter her roll before I can present her to my family over dinner. My future looks better and better. She'll be tortured by everything, and I'll be amused —watching her pay me back for all the suffering she's put me through.

I stand up and shower after my steam. I get out, dry off, and pull on my silk pajama bottoms. Walking back into my room, I see it's only going on 9 p.m. I decide to have a nightcap before bed, needing something to calm my nerves due to having her in my house. Not only does she tease me by simply being present, but I'm also on edge—worrying she'll burn the place down with a scented candle or some shit. That reminds me . . . new rule: no candles in my house.

I head to the kitchen and pull the bottle of scotch from the cabinet. I take down a glass and pour in the liquid before tossing it back and deciding on another. I pull out my phone, tempted to send a text to my best friend, Foster, to see if he wants to go grab a drink. It's been five minutes of her living here and I already need to get out. I decide against texting Foster and grab the bottle of scotch. As I'm pouring my second drink, she steps into the kitchen and we both freeze when our eyes land on each other.

She's wearing a long, oversized T-shirt that hangs down to her mid-thigh. I can't see any shorts beneath, and that nearly makes my dick jump. Her auburn hair is long and dark—soaking wet as it hangs down on either side of her face. Her face is free of makeup, but her lips look plump and her eyes are almost doe-like.

"Oh, sorry. I didn't realize you were in here. I was just grabbing some water before bed." She points toward the fridge.

"Help yourself," I insist. I step to the side, taking the bottle and glass with me.

She rounds the island in the center of the kitchen and opens the glass door of the fridge, taking out a bottle of water. I can't help but notice the way that shirt rides up slightly when she reaches for the bottle. She closes the fridge and turns to leave, but stops at the doorway. She turns back to face me, her eyes downcast. "Sorry about dinner tonight." She shakes her head once and squares her chin. "You're just really good at pissing me off."

I smirk. "Ditto," I agree. "Good night, Poppy." I raise my glass to her and she turns and leaves me alone, staring after her round ass as it sways back and forth under that thin piece of material.

She's going to fucking kill me. If not with her words, then with her body I'm not allowed to touch.

Sleep comes easily, but it's not dreamless. She takes up residence in each dream, forcing her way into my head—almost like I've forced my way into her life. The dreams start out looking a lot like the time we've spent together: arguing and fighting over whatever stupid issue is at hand. In the first dream, we fight over our living arrangement. In the second dream, we fight over who's preparing dinner, which I find extremely weird since I have a chef. Slowly but surely, the dreams begin morphing into something else entirely. The fighting stops and a friendship grows. That friendship blossoms into love, which leads to her sleeping in my bed with my arms around her, holding her close to my body and feeling relaxed as I breathe in her scent.

Her body is on top of mine, kissing my neck as she frees me from my pants. Burning heat greets me as she slides down my length, wrapping me up in her taut body. My hands find her hips as her tongue tangles against mine. I can already feel my release rising to the surface and making itself known. She lets out a breathy moan that has me coming undone in ways I never have before. Just as my release rises to the surface, my alarm clock goes off and my eyes pop open.

I'm breathing hard and my forehead is peppered with sweat. I look down my body to make sure she isn't actually there, even though I know it's impossible. The bed and the room are completely empty of everything but me. I drop my head back down onto my pillow and work to control my racing heart. After a few seconds of letting that dream slip away, I shut off the alarm and push myself out of bed, going directly into the bathroom to shower for work.

I'd hoped that the shower would help my body relax from the uneasiness of that dream. However, I find myself more and more aggravated. I've always had an itch for Poppy, but we're so different that most of the time, the need for her is forgotten under a bed of arguments and irritation. I was hoping that bringing her into my house and forcing her to play this role would only help that need get pushed further back in my mind. Unfortunately, all it did was bring her to the forefront. Based on that dream, my need for her has only grown. I can no longer ignore that itch. My head dips forward, allowing the water to wash over it. I try pushing all thoughts of her away, but my body betrays me. I'm aching and ready for release. Even with the discipline and control over my own body and mind, I can't force it down—not even with thoughts of baseball and granny panties.

With a sigh of disappointment, I take myself in hand, working from the tip to my shaft as quickly and aggressively as possible. I try to keep my mind clear as I take care of this problem before it turns into a problem I have all day long. But my self-control is clearly slipping, because even though I started out clearheaded, I'm soon only thinking of her and that dream. I remember her heat as she lowered herself onto me. I remember her hot, soft body pressed against mine, the way she kissed me with so much power and passion, and the way her fingers threaded into my hair—pulling it as small gasps slipped between her lips and mine. It doesn't take long before I'm emptying myself on the shower floor and letting all my irritation wash down the drain.

A pang of guilt eats at me, but mostly, it's the aggravation I feel regarding this whole mess. I wonder if Daniel was right. Do I only want her because she's the only one I can't have? If that's the case, then why *can't* I have her? I mean, look at me. I'm a young, wealthy, good-looking, healthy guy. Any woman would be proud to have me in her bed for an evening. But with Poppy, it isn't about the money or power. I wonder what it is that drives her. What is it that she finds attractive in a man? Surely there's *something* I can offer.

I dress and step out of my room, going to the dining room for coffee and breakfast. I sit at my usual seat and pick up the paper while my house manager, Jane, pours my coffee and fixes my plate.

"What would you like today, sir?" she asks as she dumps creamer into my cup.

I glance at the selection on the table. "I'll take some eggs, fruit, and oatmeal please."

She fixes a plate and places it in front of me as I scan the paper.

My attention is pulled away from my paper when movement

catches my eye. I turn my head and find Poppy walking into the dining room, dressed and ready.

"Well, maybe you can be on time after all," I tease.

She offers up a small smile. "I tried." She shrugs carelessly.

"Please, sit and have some breakfast. We still have a few minutes before we have to go."

She moves to the same chair she took last night and begins making her plate as Jane pours her coffee. "This is crazy. All of this food is for you?" she asks, bringing a piece of bacon to her mouth and taking a bite.

Oh, what I wouldn't do to be that piece of bacon right now. I nod. "For us."

"This is wasteful. They cook like this every morning?"

"They do."

"So what happens to the leftovers?"

I frown. She worries about the silliest things. "It's not wasteful, I have them cook this much because they take it to the homeless shelter over on 53rd." I can see the shock on her face. "Didn't know I had a philanthropic heart, did you? Hard to probably see past all that prejudice you have against the wealthy." I know I shouldn't, but I can't help myself.

She rolls her eyes and shakes her head. "You should have them donate all that crystal to the homeless as well."

I snort. "And what would the homeless need crystal for?" I know what she means, but I'm just goading her.

Her eyebrows shoot up. "Uh, sell it, obviously, and actually put the money to good use instead of letting it collect dust."

"Would it kill you to just eat and not argue?"

"Would it kill you to put that wealth and power to good use?" she throws back, and for once, I'm speechless.

My mouth opens to reply, but it snaps shut and my jaw flexes as I shake my head. "Jane?" I call.

She quickly appears in the doorway. "Yes, sir?"

"Per Poppy's request, would you and the staff mind packing up the crystal and putting it up for auction at Christie's? Donate the proceeds to the shelter, please."

"Uh, um, no sir, I guess not," she finally gets out.

I look back at Poppy. "Happy now?"

She smiles. "Very. See, that wasn't hard, now was it?"

FIVE

POPPY

I t didn't take long for me to fall into a deep sleep in that big, fluffy bed. But even in my sleep, Matthew's presence haunted me. It's getting harder and harder to avoid my attraction to him. But in my dreams, he doesn't talk or act the way he does in real life. In my dreams, he's nice, polite, charming, and outgoing. So when he tells me I'm beautiful and pulls me against him, I don't fight him. I kiss him. The soft kiss turns heated, and before I know it, he's throwing me up against the wall and kissing his way down my body. His lips are hot against my neck, nearly burning a trail to my lower belly.

His hands push my dress up my thighs as he falls to his knees, bringing his mouth to my drenched sex. I feel his hot tongue slip between my slick folds as my breathing picks up. My entire body hardens as he's pushing me closer to the edge. Just as my release rises, my eyes pop open and I let out a groan.

I find myself overly irritated from the dream. I'm pissed at myself for letting my unconscious mind go there—having dream sex with a man I loathe. I'm mad that my body is now on high alert and needs to be worked over and reset. But most of all, I hate that I wish it were real. I wish I could feel his body moving against mine. I hate that I'm jealous of all the women who have gotten to take what they wanted while I'm stuck denying my attraction to him. And I hate that he isn't the man from my fantasies—a man who's caring, giving, and easygoing. And even though I know all of this, I hate that I can't control the way my body reacts to him.

I throw back the blankets and go to cool off in the shower. My alarm hasn't even gone off yet, but I'm too frustrated to sleep any longer. My body feels tense and sore—like I didn't relax a moment last night. I have a dull headache, probably from overthinking that dream, and I feel irritable, like I can't quite get a handle on my mood today. That will probably make the day go by that much more slowly, and there's no doubt it will cause some fights between us.

After washing off, I climb out and get started on my hair, makeup, and getting dressed. I get ready remarkably fast and find myself pacing the floor in my room. I wanted to be late again today as a way to get to him, but there's nothing for me to do in here, and the smell of breakfast is too good. It lures me out, and I find him sitting in the dining room.

I make my bowl of oatmeal topped with fruit while Jane pours me a nasty cup of coffee. "Would it be too much to ask for a glass of orange juice?" I ask her sweetly as she sets down the carafe.

"No problem at all. One moment, please." She leaves the room.

"Not a coffee person?" Matthew asks.

I wrinkle my nose. "I can't stand the stuff. For one, I'm not big on drinking hot stuff, but I also can't stand the overly-sweet or bitter stuff anyway."

Jane is back and setting a glass on the table.

"Jane, from now on, Poppy will take orange juice for breakfast, not coffee."

She offers a bow. "Yes, sir."

I give him a small smile as a way to say *thank you*, but I find this whole setup weird. His life is so different in comparison to mine. I'm not used to bathtubs deep enough to drown in, someone waiting on me hand and foot, and finding that the clothing I left on the bathroom floor has been magically laundered and put away. I'm used to sniffing the clothes on the floor to see if they're clean or dirty, using paper plates in order to avoid washing dishes, and actually having to get up and do things for myself.

We don't talk as I eat and he reads the paper, but when he starts to fold it back up, I figure it's time to leave. I quickly finish up break-fast and stand, holding my dirty dishes in my hand to take to the sink.

"Poppy, please just leave that. There are people who get paid good money to clean up around here. It's not your job."

"Oh, right," I mumble, setting everything back down.

"Are you ready to go?"

I nod, smoothing down my black skirt.

I suck in a breath when I feel his hand pressing on the small of my back, motioning for me to walk ahead of him with the other. There's a painless burning sensation under his hand and I find it taking over my whole body as I push myself forward. My legs suddenly feel weak, like jello, and my heart and lungs are racing. We stop at the door and pull on our coats, neither of us looking at the other. I sneak a glance when he's not looking and see that it appears he's breathing a little harder too, but maybe it's just due to the walk to the door mixed with the excitement of leaving the house for the day. I'm sure it's nothing. He's not attracted to me. Why would he be? He's rich and can have literally any girl he wants—one that his uppity family would approve of, who would actually listen when he gave a demand. I push those thoughts from my mind as he opens the door and holds it, allowing me to walk out first.

I'm not sure what to expect on the drive to the office, and I'm a little nervous thinking about it. He climbs behind the wheel and starts the car. He places his briefcase between my left leg and the dash before pulling on his seatbelt. He moves slowly and carefully, almost like he's hyperaware of me being at his side. He adjusts the heat and the vents, then finally shifts into drive. He takes off slowly, but he has a wrinkle between his brows as he steers out of the parking garage.

"We talked about our upbringing last night. Why don't we move on to something a little easier . . . like what do you like to do in your spare time? What are your hobbies and interests?" he asks.

That sounds like an easy topic that can't cause too much of a fuss, right? "Well, I like to read romance novels." I roll my eyes because what woman doesn't? But he scoffs.

"What?" I ask, turning my head to study him.

"Romance novels? Seriously?"

"What's wrong with that?"

"Nothing, if you want to live your life being let down because real men don't stand a chance next to the fictional characters you're dreaming about."

I laugh. "Oh, we know real men can't compete. That's why we read them. It's nice to dream, right?"

He shrugs. "I prefer to dream about things that may actually happen one day."

"Like what? What do you dream about that can happen in real life?"

He keeps his eyes on the road. "I don't know. Finding love—real love. Not someone who's only interested in my money or social status. Getting married, starting a family . . . the classic dream, I guess."

"Well, I suppose all that's good, but don't you like to imagine? To just let your thoughts carry you away into something you know isn't possible? I mean, dreaming is the only way you can experience those things."

He glances at me from the corner of his eye. "I guess we're just two very different people. I prefer to keep things real while you like spending your time in la-la land."

I snort. "How is it possible for two people to be so different?" I ask, but he doesn't answer, and that effectively ends our conversation.

We make it to the office and Matthew and I are walking in together just as Daniel walks out of his office. He smirks. "Poppy, it's nice to see you again so soon after your recent . . . *outburst*," he says with a chuckle.

I frown at him. "Did you have something to do with this?" I ask, putting my hand on my hip as I study him.

"I'm not sure what you mean," he says as his eyes move from Matthew, to me, and back.

Matthew brushes past him. "Daniel, do you mind if we talk in my office?"

"Sure," Daniel agrees, looking at me as if he's trying to figure out what the hell is going on around here.

He turns and heads into the office, leaving me alone to get things started for the day. I turn on my phone as my computer boots up, then I start pulling files. To my surprise, there aren't a ton of emails from him with lists of things to do, but I guess I kept him pretty busy last night between the move, dinner, and our argument. Maybe he just didn't have time to work. So while I wait, I decide to clean up around the office—wiping down the coffee station, cleaning the public restroom, and taking out the trash.

When lunch rolls around, I'm surprised when he leaves his office and stops at my desk. "Ready?" he asks.

"Ready for . . . ?" I let my sentence drop off. He's never come to my desk to leave his lunch order. He's always made me go to him.

"To go to lunch. I have reservations."

"Oh. For the both of us?" I ask, still confused.

He lets out a deep chuckle. "Of course. I'll take any excuse I can get to spend time with my fiancée throughout the day."

Oh, I see. He's just wanting to do more interrogation. But whatever. At least I get to leave the office to enjoy some fancy rich-people food. I grab my purse and follow him to the door. I'm pleasantly surprised when he opens it and allows me to walk through first. "Thank you," I say, passing by him.

He takes ahold of my elbow and guides me across the street to the parking garage. At his car, he opens my door and allows me to slide inside. Finally, he climbs behind the wheel.

"Okay, what's going on? Are you trying to trick me or something?" I ask, suddenly waiting for the ball to drop.

He looks at me, confused. "What are you talking about?"

"This." I motion between us. "You're never this nice to me. So what's up?"

He takes a deep breath and starts the car. "I just figured that if I really want to pull this off and sell that we're a real couple, we need to get to know one another. And being assholes to each other is only going to hinder that. We need to put our egos aside and get to business."

"And by *get to business* you mean . . . ?"

He scoffs and rolls his eyes, clearly annoyed that I'm not keeping up with the conversation. "I mean we need to treat each other better. Get comfortable as a couple so we don't have to try so hard when we're in public. This is our test. If we can get along throughout lunch —look like a real couple in love who are about to get married—then this just might work."

I press my lips together and nod. "Okay. If you can stop being an ass, then so can I," I promise.

He chuckles. "Are you sure about that?"

I snort. "Are you?" I challenge.

He only laughs harder. "We're doomed. You can't be outdone and I won't be outdone."

I smile, glad he's already learned a little about me. But as we make our way to the restaurant, this idea of his worries me. I mean, what if we *can* pull off the fake relationship thing? Will the lines get blurred? And where does the relationship end and our regular lives begin—especially now that we're living in the same house and eating three meals a day together? But on the other hand, it will give me a reason to touch him and tease myself even further. So maybe it won't be so bad after all.

I decide to try this relationship thing before we even get to the restaurant. His hand is resting on the console between us. I lift my hand and slide it into his. His eyes immediately jump to me.

I smile and shrug. "Just wanted to see how it would feel. You know . . . if I'd be able to fake it or if I'd feel repulsed."

He smirks. "And? How does it feel?"

I force my eyes to the road, refusing to let him see the pink that's staining my cheeks. "It feels . . . different, but nice."

He squeezes slightly. "It will take some getting used to, but I think I can manage as well."

We hold hands for the rest of the drive, and that teenage girl inside me squeals with delight—like it's the first time she's ever been touched by the opposite sex.

SIX

MATTHEW

Her hand is soft in mine—warm, trusting, inviting. It only makes me think about how inviting the rest of her body is. Would she allow me to wrap my arm around her? Would she shy away if I reached out and ran the tip of my finger across her cheek? Would she allow me to kiss her? To touch her in ways neither of us should want? Only time will tell, but even this light touch is enough to have me wondering and looking forward to finding out more.

We arrive at the restaurant and I get out of the car, allowing the valet to take a seat behind the wheel. I walk around the car and Poppy is already opening her door, but I hold out my arm and she takes it. I close the door and lead her inside. I almost feel giddy having her on my arm. It's like I'm back in high school and got the most popular girl to go to prom with me. Dare I say, I'm even proud to have her next to me. But that confuses my mind in ways I don't understand, so I push the emotion away as I lead her up to the hostess.

"Reservation for two under Lewis."

She looks over the book. "Ah, found it. Right this way, Mr.

Lewis." She grabs two menus and leads us in the direction of our table.

She places us in a semi-private back corner. It's far enough away that not many people will notice us, but it's also open enough that we're not secluded from the rest of the diners. I pull out a chair and offer it to Poppy. She takes it and I help her slide it forward before taking my place across from her.

"Here's the wine list; your waiter will be with you shortly," the hostess tells us.

"Would you like wine with lunch?" I ask her, but she shakes her head.

"I don't drink much, especially if I have to go back to work. I'm a bit of a lightweight when it comes to holding my alcohol."

I set the list aside and look over my menu to decide what I'd like to eat.

The waiter approaches our table. He looks down at me with no pad of paper. "What would you like to get started?"

"I'll take a scotch on the rocks." I realize drinking hard liquor midday isn't smart and something I seldom—if ever—do, but I need to relax. This woman has me on edge, and my anxiety is through the roof.

"And you, ma'am?" he asks, looking over at her. I can't help but notice the way his eyes bug out of his skull slightly when he takes her in. That's weird. I never considered Poppy to be the obviously sexy type. I didn't realize the effect she had on men. I thought I was only attracted to her because she hated me so fervently, but maybe it's more than that.

"I'll just take a water with lemon, please."

He nods. "Very well. Would you like a basket of rolls while you wait?"

"No," I say at the same time Poppy says, "Yes, please."

The two of us look at each other. The waiter is clearly confused and finally says, "I'll bring a basket." He walks away.

"Why are you turning down free bread?" she asks.

"Why are you accepting free carbs?" I reply.

There's a long moment in which the two of us are just squaring off, not talking. Then she rolls her eyes and her back relaxes. "Fine."

Our drinks arrive along with a basket of rolls that remains untouched.

"Oh, I have something for you," I say, reaching into my breast pocket and handing over an envelope.

"What is it?" she asks around a wide smile, almost like she's surprised I'm giving her a gift.

She opens the envelope and pulls out the contents. A gym card, a business card with her trainer's information and schedule, and a copy of her calendar for the next month. I've already taken the liberty of filling it in for her. Gym three times a week, etiquette classes so she can learn the proper ways things should be done in high society, and appointments to get her hair, nails, and body groomed properly.

"What's all this?" she asks, examining everything.

"Not to start an argument or anything, but a woman who's preparing to be my fiancée needs to take better care of herself. So I took the liberty of getting you a gym membership and I've booked you with a trainer three nights a week. I've also set up appointments for you to get a manicure and pedicure, a haircut, and a full-body wax along with a massage. I'm not demanding you do these things—just letting you know you have access."

She presses her lips together and nods. "And this?" she holds up the reservation for the tea time during which she will be learning etiquette with other young ladies.

"It was just a guess, but I figured you didn't know what all the forks were for on the table. That, and my family will tear you apart at dinner. The more prepared you can be, the better."

"Seriously? Your family cares which fork I use?" Her voice pitches to an octave only dogs can hear. "What, are we on the *Titanic?*" she snorts, clearly amusing herself. I don't respond. Instead,

I just take a deep breath and level my eyes at her once again so she can see the seriousness in my expression. High society isn't a joke and it still exists in America.

She nods and slips everything back into the envelope. "And when is the shopping trip? I don't see that on here."

"What shopping trip?" I ask, suddenly confused.

"If I remember correctly, you tossed one of my bags out the window. I had clothes and shoes in there. And it was stuff I wear frequently. Plus I don't have gym clothes . . . unless you want me working out in the T-shirts and panties I sleep in."

My dick twitches. So I was right. No shorts were under that shirt of hers.

I clear my throat. "We'll go this weekend. The gym schedule starts next week. Every Sunday, Tuesday, and Thursday."

She smiles and nods, but then she reaches across the table and places her hand in mine. "And I can only assume that in order to sell this to your family, I'll need an engagement ring of some kind."

"I already have my jeweler coming by this evening so I can pick out your ring."

"Oh, the jewelry comes to you? Nice," she agrees.

I smile. I want to threaten her within an inch of her life if she loses the ring, but I don't say anything, because she's playing so well right now that I don't want to ruin it. I wish we'd been seated in a booth so I could hold her against my side and see how far she'd let me take this.

The waiter is back. "Are you ready to place your order?"

I hand over my menu. "Yes, we'll both take the lunch special."

"Okay, which soup?"

"We'll have the minestrone with the house salad, please."

He nods. "As you wish." He takes both menus and walks away.

I can see the fight in her eyes from me ordering for us both, and I watch, waiting to see if she'll be able to hold her tongue or not.

"So, where were we on getting to know each other?" she asks with a flirty smile.

I can't help but play along, pretending it's real. I smile at her. "What are your favorite kinds of movies?"

"Hmm," she says, thinking it over. "I guess I like scary movies. It gives people the excuse to get close." Again with the teasing grin.

I chuckle. "You're good at this."

"Good at what?" she asks, batting her lashes.

"Flirting. If I didn't know better, I'd think you actually liked me."

She shrugs one shoulder. "I'm a good actress. Plus, getting to know you a little better does help. You're not entirely the fuckboy I thought you were, but there's still plenty of room for improvement."

I laugh. "Are you trying to train me?"

"Nope. I'm just trying to make this as smooth as possible."

The waiter comes out with our soups and salads and she releases my hand to eat. I already miss it there. I wish I could treat her like I would any other girl I'd normally date, but that's not how we are and that's not the type of relationship we have . . . although she *is* a good actress and she even has me wondering if it's all acting or if she could be feeling the same for me as I am for her.

———

THE WORKWEEK GOES by without a hitch. She's completely different now that we're living together. She's never late and she seems to have her shit together at work, though I suppose I've also been trying to take it a little easier on her.

Friday after work, I present her with a dress for dinner with my grandmother. It's a black number that's made out of thin black material covered in sheer lace. It's a form-fitting dress with tiny little sleeves. The dress ends just below the knee, but the tightness of the dress leaves very little to the imagination. I give her a pair of matching sky-high black heels that give a nice shape to her legs. I've also included a matching purse and jewelry.

"So, what do you think?" she asks, spinning in a circle before me.

I wet my lips, ready to eat her up. "I think you look great," I say, not wanting to give her too much to have her worrying about the meaning behind it. I pull the ring out of my pocket. "Here's the engagement ring I promised. I went ahead and took care of it without you. Now, this is only a loaner and it's worth about $20,000, so *do not lose it*. In fact, don't even wear it unless we're going to a family function. Got it?"

She nods but rolls her eyes like she can't believe I don't trust her with such a priceless item. I open the box and show her the ring, causing her eyes to widen in shock. It's a platinum halo with a pear diamond in the center.

"This is gorgeous," she breathes out.

I take it out of the box and slide it onto her finger. "Will you be my pretend fiancée?" I smirk.

"Yes!" She plays along, jumping and wrapping her arms around my neck. I laugh at her theatrics, but place her on her feet.

Even though she's standing on her own now, her arms don't pull away from my neck. I pull back, putting us eye-to-eye, and we both freeze.

Her red lips are glistening and parted as her breathing picks up. I can feel the charge of electricity bouncing between us. I wonder if she can too, but then I remember how breathless she seems, so I think it's safe to say she does. That or this is just a little too close for comfort and she's feeling worried or scared. I wish I could read her mind. Maybe then I'd know what to do. I'm torn between leaning in and kissing her, and pulling back and keeping this game going between us.

Part of me knows, though, that if I *do* lean in and kiss her, I won't want to stop. And even if she lets it go on, we won't make it to dinner. If she stops it, dinner will be unbearable until we can finally clear the air. So I clear my throat, breaking the moment between us. Her arms fall back to her sides and I'm finally allowed to take a step back.

"We should probably get going," I say, holding out my elbow.

"Of course," she breathes out, nodding her head. As we make our way to the door, it seems like she's trying to keep herself under control. Her hands are shaking slightly and her legs are wobbly like they're weak. I wonder if this is her natural reaction to being in my arms. The thought makes me smirk with pleasure. Maybe I'm not as far off from getting what I want after all.

SEVEN

POPPY

I don't know what that was, but I nearly blew my cover. He presented me with the ring and I wanted to play along like it was a real engagement. I said yes and leapt into his arms. He laughed and hugged me tightly, but when he pulled away, I didn't want to let go. Maybe I got caught up in the performance, but deep down I know it had nothing to do with that. My reaction *was* my natural reaction to him. Even though I've always been attracted to him, spending all this time together has only made that attraction grow. I guess if he brings it up, I could just play it off like it was just part of the game.

We get into the car and he addresses the issue more quickly than I thought he would. "What was that back there?"

"What was what?" I ask, pretending like I have no idea what he's talking about.

"It . . . it seemed like you wanted me to kiss you." His voice is soft, unsure, nervous. It's so far off from the way he usually sounds—sure and full of authority.

I laugh it off. "It was just a quick thought. Caught up in the moment, ya know?"

"So you did want me to kiss you?" he asks, still confused.

"I mean, not for real. I was just thinking that it's probably something we need to work on, you know? How will anyone buy us as a couple if we never touch or kiss? And if we do end up kissing in front of someone—you know, for the show of it all—they'll know right away that we're not really together if we have no chemistry and end up stumbling through our first kiss."

"Oh, so it's all in the name of research and practice then?"

"Well, what else would it be for? I mean, you hate me with a passion and I can't stand you most days," I lie. Well, I guess it's only a half-lie. Before this arrangement, I couldn't stand him most days, but now as we get closer, I find myself liking him more and more, especially after he asked his staff to donate the crystal. And it seems the more time we spend together, the more he's working to control his tone of voice, his anger, and the way he words certain things. He hasn't insulted me all day. That has to mean something, right? Thinking back on that almost-kiss, it seemed like for a split second, he wanted to kiss me too. But just as I was confused about it all, I think he was too.

We pull into the driveway of an unbelievably large house. This place has brick walls around it with an iron gate, a circle drive in front of the house, and a fountain in the center. The lawn is perfectly manicured and the walkways are lined with complementary flowers and shrubbery. Matthew pulls up to the front door and stops the car. I'm too busy staring up at the mansion.

"Poppy?" he says my name.

"Huh?" I ask, not pulling my gaze from the house. I'm almost expecting to see gargoyles perched on top. So his family *does* have a Bruce Wayne-style estate. Naturally.

"Poppy?" he says it again.

I turn my head toward him this time. I don't know what's happening to me, but seeing him in the darkness of the car, with the blue dash lights lighting up his face, he takes my breath away. His high cheekbones are prominent, his jaw sharp, and his lips plump and soft—teasing. His dark eyes are what really draw me in though.

They're wide and fully alert, but it's like they hold so many secrets, and the only way to get answers is by diving into the murky water.

"I know you're probably over there freaking out right now, but just try to relax. My father isn't here tonight. It's just my grandmother, and she's always kind. Well, mostly. She can be a real spitfire when she needs to be," he jokes, turning off the car and opening his door.

I'm momentarily lost. Did he just reassure me? That isn't something he would've done a few days ago. Before, he would've enjoyed watching me worry and squirm. Something is changing between us, and more than anything, it worries me. What if I actually fall for this new guy he's becoming?

He opens my door and the movement makes me jump after being so lost in my thoughts. He holds out his hand and I slide mine into it. His warm skin is there to greet me with comfort, and it causes a fire to spread from my hand to my lower belly.

Whoa, body. Chill the fuck out. This is only pretend.

He leads me to the door and presses the doorbell. Only seconds later, it's being opened by a maid dressed in a black and white uniform. "Good evening," she greets us.

"Good evening, Rose," he replies, stepping inside and dragging me in with him.

He shrugs out of his coat then moves behind me to help with mine. He hands them both over to her. "Rose, this is my fiancée, Poppy. Poppy, this is Rose. She's worked for my grandmother since I was just a boy."

I hold out my hand to shake. "It's nice to meet you."

She smiles and nods. "You too, dear." She closes the front door. "Your grandmother is in the lounge."

"Thank you, Rose." Matthew takes my hand and wraps it around his elbow as he leads me to the lounge. We enter the room, and to my surprise, it's just a living room. There are two couches facing each other, with a chair on either end of them and a table in the middle. There's a warm and inviting fireplace with a fire burning inside, and a drink cart off to the side. There are also decorative pieces around the room, but I have a feeling the seating area is meant to be the focal point, meant purely for entertaining.

The old lady is sitting in the chair next to the fireplace and she looks to be about 200 years old. She's a tiny thing—so small it looks like she won't even be able to bear her own weight if she stands. Her graying hair is thinning on top, so much so that I can see her scalp, but she has it pulled back into a slick bun atop her head. She's dressed in a long-sleeved black dress that's probably as old as she is. She's pale and looks to be nearly falling asleep—that is, until she notices us walking into the room. Her eyes pop wide open and a soft smile plays on her thin, dry lips.

"Good evening, Nan," Matthew says, releasing my arm and going to lean over to press a kiss to her head. "I'd like to introduce you to my fiancée. This is Poppy."

I smile as I move closer with my hand outstretched, ready to shake.

"Fiancée?" she questions, looking up at him.

"That's right," he agrees.

"You're getting married? Finally? Oh, this is good news." She turns her attention to me now. "What a beautiful woman you are," she says, raising her hand to shake.

I take it gently, almost afraid of hurting the woman. "Thank you," I reply. "It's nice to finally meet you. I've heard so much about you that I feel like I know you already," I lie.

She blushes as she tears her gaze from mine to look up at Matthew. "Matthew, you haven't been telling this beautiful fiancée of yours lies about me, now have you?"

He chuckles as he walks around her to sit on the sofa, motioning for me to join him. "I may have told her a few things—but lies, no way."

I take a seat next to him and cross my legs so my knees are pointing toward him. My right foot touches the back of his calf, and with her eyes on us, I feel like I need to sell this a little better.

I run my foot up and down the back of his leg as I take his hand in mine.

"Well, your father can't be here tonight, as usual. He will make brunch, though, on Sunday. Poppy, will you be joining us?"

I smile. "Oh, I don't know. I haven't been invited."

"Well, dear. I'm inviting you. Ten sharp," she insists. "This marriage will be a big family affair and you need to meet your soon-to-be father-in-law. James will be thrilled. Have you told him yet?"

"Not yet. I thought it best to do it in person. I wasn't sure what his reaction would be," Matthew says, squeezing my hand.

"Of course he'll be happy, Matthew. Have you set a date yet?" she asks, smoothing her gray hair back.

"Not yet," I answer. "It only just happened and I need to hire a coordinator. We'll send you a save-the-date card as soon as we have them. You're first on the list."

She offers a weak smile and nods.

I look for any sign that she's unwell, but all I can see is that she's old—really, really old. It makes me wonder if her body is shutting down rather than her actually being sick with something. Other than being tiny and weak-looking, she seems perfectly healthy to me, but I guess we can't always see what's going on behind the scenes.

"Dinner is ready, Mrs. Lewis," the maid pops her head in and says.

"Well, looks like we'd better get up then." She uncrosses her ankles and holds on to the arms of the chair. She pushes herself upward, but her knees give slightly and Matthew has to put his hand on her arm, helping her stand. Slowly, at her pace, we leave the lounge area and move into the formal dining room.

She takes her seat at the head of the table with Matthew and me on either side of her. The maid starts to bring the food from the kitchen, putting a serving on each of our plates as she makes her way around the table. By the time she's done, I have a small side salad, roast with potatoes and carrots, a dinner roll, and some fancy-looking green beans. Wine is poured into a glass in front of me and I notice there's no water or anything else to drink. Looks like I'll be getting tipsy tonight. At least tomorrow is Saturday and I don't have to work, but I do have a full spa and shopping day planned.

I stay as quiet as I can throughout dinner, letting Matthew have his time with his grandmother. I only ever talk if one of them asks me a direct question. I eat my dinner and have to wash it down with the wine. By the end of the glass, I already feel sparkly and happy. My face is warm and everything seems funny, but I know I have to control myself.

Our plates are cleared and I'm thinking we'll finally get to head home, but no. More food is brought out and put in front of me—some kind of pudding that looks to be slightly toasted. There are graham crackers sticking out of it and it smells sweet and delicious. I can eat the dessert, no problem, but I'm concerned about the brandy glasses they're now placing on the table. My eyes leap up to Matthew and he sees the panic written all over my face. However, he must have a quick flash back to his old self, because all he does is smile my way, knowing exactly how I feel.

Dessert starts and I dip my spoon into the pudding and take a small bite. It's sweet, light, and fluffy. It's not something I've had before, but it's really good.

"Try it with the brandy, dear. It makes it all the better," his grandmother insists.

I force a smile as I reach forward and pick up the glass. I take a sip and the alcohol burns my throat, but it brings out the sweetness in the pudding and it really does pull everything together. To my surprise, I eat the entire dessert and drink almost the whole glass of brandy.

Being this drunk and sitting this still is hard to do. I find myself spacing out as they talk—taking in the room more than paying attention to the conversation. I giggle to myself as I imagine the plates and candlesticks dancing around on the table singing "Be Our Guest." This place could be straight out of *Beauty and the Beast*.

It feels like it takes forever, but dinner finally ends and the two of them stand in front of the table. My eyes jump up to Matthew. I cautiously push back my chair and stand, testing the strength of my legs as I hold on to the edge of the table. I turn and walk back toward the door slowly and carefully. At the end of the table, Matthew places his hand around my arm, steadying me.

He helps me to the door, keeping his hand on me to keep me steady. He helps me with my coat and we say our goodbyes to his grandmother. When the door closes behind us, I let out a long, dragged-out breath. He chuckles beside me.

"God, I thought it'd never end. What time is it?"

"Nine," he answers without having to look at the time.

I look up at the moon. "How do you know that?" I'm trying to figure out if he can tell time by the sky like the ancient Romans did.

He laughs. "Dinner always ends at 9 p.m. You weren't lying when you said you can't handle your alcohol, were you?"

I laugh, a snort slipping out. "No, not at all. That was more than I've ever imbibed at once."

"What? What did you do for your 21st birthday then?"

"I stayed home and hung out with some friends. I don't drink," I nearly slur. I thought standing would help sober me up, but it seems the more time that passes, the more drunk I become. He opens the door for me and helps me inside. The interior of the car is dark and warm and soothing. I lean my head back and my lids get heavy.

EIGHT

MATTHEW

She falls asleep before I even get out of the driveway. I can't help but snicker at her head that's lolled to the side, her lips parted with her deep, heavy breathing. I can't believe she got so wasted off one glass of wine and a sip of brandy. Okay, maybe it was more than a sip, but it wasn't what I would consider a glass. My grandmother is 80-something years old and she likes her brandy, but she also has a limit. What she served tonight was her limit. Dinner ends when it does because that's how long it takes her to get drunk. When 9 p.m. hits, she wants to be buzzed and in bed. If Poppy wasn't so drunk herself, she might have noticed it.

My phone vibrates in my pocket and I see it's Foster calling me. I slip my Bluetooth earbuds in and answer his call, "Hey man, what's up?"

"Dude, where you been? You've blown off our last two poker nights and you missed Bret's bachelor party."

"Sorry, man, work has been crazy." I glance over at Poppy and contemplate saying something about her, then decide against it.

"Well, I'm coming over tomorrow night and we're catching up. I need to fill you in on what went down at Bret's bachelor party. There was this strip—"

"I'm seeing someone," I blurt out before he can finish his statement. I don't know why I blurted it out, but the cat's out of the bag now.

"What the fuck? Well, spill," he says.

"Not tonight, man, but we'll go out soon. I promise." We say goodbye and I try to figure out what I'm going to tell him about Poppy. Foster knows what it's like to have certain expectations placed on you from birth. We were both raised by rich tyrant fathers—only his took things a step further and promised him to Bianca Harris before he was even born. According to his dad, it's a way to merge their empires. Too bad his dad hasn't even considered what Foster wants in life.

I finish the drive home and Poppy never wakes. When I pull into the garage, she still doesn't stir. "Poppy, we're here," I say rather loudly, but she doesn't move an inch.

I let out a deep breath as I shift into park and turn off the car. I get out, moving around the back and opening her door. "Poppy?" I try again, but nothing.

Not knowing what else to do, I reach in and pick her up against me. I push the door shut with my hip and walk with her in my arms to the elevator. The ride is smooth and I take the moment to enjoy the weight and heat of her body against mine. As the doors slide open, I walk inside and move toward the couch to lay her down. I plan on moving her to her bedroom eventually, but I need to rest my arms for a moment first.

I go to lay her down and her eyes flicker open. I freeze as our eyes lock—painful arms now forgotten. Her eyes seem darker than usual and they're drawing me into their depths. Her tongue comes out, wetting her lips and making them glisten with the fire burning in the fireplace. That charge of electricity is back and bouncing between us rapidly, drawing my lips closer to hers.

It happens so fast that I don't even realize it's happening until it's too late. She closes the space between us, pressing her lips to mine. A sudden fire ignites in my lips and scorches them, making its way down my throat and to my belly, where an explosion happens. Her tongue tangles with mine as our lips move perfectly in sync. I breathe her in—the scent of lilac and jasmine mixing with the brandy on her breath creates a delicious mixture I could easily get lost in. As my body comes alive with this kiss, my arms feel like they're about to fall off. I lay her down on the couch and cover her body with mine, never breaking the kiss.

Lying down only makes everything seem that much better. The soft kiss turns to one of passion as her arms wrap around my neck. Her legs part, moving to either side of my hips. I can feel the heat of her center radiating toward me, welcoming me like a thick wool blanket. My body comes alive in ways I haven't felt in many years.

Sure, I've been with many women these last couple years, but none of them had her appeal. I never wanted them as badly as I want her. Every touch feels like an explosion on my skin. Every whimper is like a magical note that brings another part of my body to life.

I'm painfully hard and pressing against her core as we kiss. I find her hips moving up and down, stroking me through our clothing. My hand moves to her hip, stilling it—not knowing how far this will go but not wanting to make it any harder on myself when it ends. Stopping her hips only makes her hands unwind from my neck—moving down to my chest, unbuttoning my shirt. I don't stop her. I don't have the willpower. I've wanted this from the first moment my eyes landed on her.

When my shirt is open, her hands find my belt and she begins to unbuckle it. I hear the clink of metal when she releases it, and it brings me back to the present. I break our kiss and move my nose to her jaw, breathing her in as I pepper her skin with soft kisses. "Poppy, we should stop," I whisper, but make no move to do so.

"Shh," she tells me. "Don't ruin it," she whispers, digging her nails into my stomach as she slides her hand down the front of my pants. Her fingers lock around my hard cock and I'm too far gone.

Her touch is like burning fire on my skin after craving it for so long. My eyes roll into the back of my head and a whimper leaves my lips as I move them back to hers. With each stroke of her hand, I feel as if I'm clinging to the side of a cliff, each stroke only making me slide down a little further no matter how deeply I dig in with my fingertips. Every muscle in my body is begging me to pick her up and carry her into my bedroom, but there's something holding me back.

Will she consider this a mistake tomorrow? Does her sober mind want this—want me? Or is this some kind of drunken confusion? Those are the only thoughts I need in order to muster the strength to do what I have to do. I break our kiss and pull away. I take her wrist in my hand and pull it off of me, in spite of how badly my body craves it. "I'm sorry, Poppy, but we can't do this. Not like this. Not tonight."

I take her hands in mine and pull her to her feet. Her eyes meet mine in the darkened living room and I can see the fire dancing in her irises. They narrow slightly, confusion pumping its way through her system. Her lips part like she's going to say something, but then she quickly snaps them shut.

She spins around and looks over her shoulder at me. "Unzip me?"

Slowly, I raise my hand to the zipper on her dress and lower it. It opens like a butterfly, giving me a full view of her back—down to the top of her ass, where I see the black lace thong she's wearing. My stomach tightens as another wave of need washes over me.

"Thank you," she whispers, taking her first step toward her room.

I stand there in the darkness alone, looking after her until she steps into her room and is no longer in sight. I hear the soft click of her door shutting, and suddenly I'm wondering if I did the right thing. I had my shot. Why didn't I take it? This whole damn ruse was nothing more than a way to watch her suffer—all while trying to get the one and only thing I wanted: her in my bed for one night. I was there. The opportunity was right in front of me and I didn't take it. Why?

I shake my head at myself. Taking her tonight would've been too easy, I tell myself. Where's the fun in that? If I'd gotten what I wanted now, there'd be no point in keeping up with this bullshit lie. I would've had my taste and been done with her. But this way, the game continues. We get to play a little longer. There's nothing wrong with letting her think she's winning for a little while, all in the name of making the game last.

I wake in the morning and have a feeling today is going to be different from the last few. I don't know exactly what I'm walking in on. Will she be happy that I stopped what was starting last night? Will she be angry that she didn't get what she wanted? Will she feel embarrassed—like I rejected her? I'm not sure, but there's only one way to find out.

I throw the blankets off and go to the bathroom to shower. I dress in a pair of jeans and a sweater. No sense in dirtying a good suit when I'm not needed in the office. I walk out of my bedroom and find her already up, dressed, and at the table. I step into the room and freeze, looking over at her. She hasn't realized I'm standing here yet as she looks intently at the newspaper. She has a little crease between her brows as she pops a grape into her mouth.

"Morning," I say, finally walking in to take my seat.

"Morning," she replies, not pulling her eyes away from the paper.

"How are you feeling today?"

"I'm fine, thanks." She still doesn't look at me and her tone is clipped—straight and to the point.

"I was a little worried last night. I've never seen someone get drunk on so little alcohol before." I wait for a reply but there is none. She only raises her eyebrows.

I make my plate and notice that hers is now completely empty. She picks up her juice and finishes it off.

"Are you finished?" I ask, picking up my fork to begin eating.

"Yes, I have a busy day. I have to get going." She folds up the paper and stands.

"Do you need a ride?" I ask, watching as she makes her way out of the dining room.

"I'll Uber. No worries. Enjoy your day." She turns to go to her room and I'm left alone.

I wasn't expecting that. I figured she'd yell at me, or bring up that she was drunk and didn't know what she was doing. I wasn't prepared to ignore last night altogether. That only leads me to believe that maybe she's embarrassed I rejected her.

I stand up and walk to her room. The door is open as she gathers her things. I knock once on the open door and she looks over at me.

"Can we talk for a moment?" I ask, walking into the room.

She shrugs. "I'm kind of in a hurry. Don't want to be late."

"It's about last night," I say, crossing my arms.

She's bending over the bed, putting her phone into her purse. She stands upright and her shoulders fall. "Do we have to? I think we both know what a mistake it would've been, and I'm glad you had the sense to stop it."

"Really?" I ask, stepping closer, feeling as if she's drawing me to her.

Her brows furrow as she watches me. "What's that supposed to mean?"

I shrug, letting my arms fall back to my sides. "I don't know. It just seems like you're hurt or embarrassed or something. And if you are, that wasn't my intention."

She snorts. "Are you apologizing because you think you hurt my feelings?" She waits but I don't answer. "There's nothing more between us than this arrangement, Matthew. I wasn't looking for more. I'm not expecting more. I was just drunk and got carried away with the pretense. I know you don't like me like that and I feel the same about you. It's a good day if we can make it a few hours together without ripping each other's heads off." She brushes past me, leaving me alone once again.

But I *do* like her like that, and I have a feeling she likes me just as much. So why keep up the charade?

NINE

POPPY

When I woke this morning, memories of last night flooded my brain. I could still taste his lips on mine and feel the heat of his body pressing against me on the couch. I could still remember the feeling of his silky softness in my hand—how hard and big he was, and how I wished we could've gone further. And even though I knew what I was doing and wanted it, I'm glad it stopped. Had it continued, I'm sure I would've fucked up and confessed my real feelings for him, and that can't happen. He doesn't see me as someone he can spend his life with. No, he sees me as the woman who beat the shit out of his expensive sports car. The one who was always late to work. The woman he hates more than anything else. This little game is his way of torturing me. He wants to see me uncomfortable under his thumb. He wants to watch me suffer just like I caused him suffering over his precious car. Getting mixed up in any other way is not acceptable.

I go outside and find my Uber waiting. I climb in the back seat and say a quick hello before popping in my AirPods, not wanting to have to deal with unnecessary chitchat. I look out the window as we speed through the city. My thoughts, as always nowadays, go back to him. Fucking Matthew Lewis III. It's still a ridiculous name no matter how good-looking he is. No matter how good of a kisser he is, no matter how big his—no, don't go there, Poppy. You're only torturing yourself. But dammit, he's such a good kisser. Not too much tongue . . . just the perfect amount. His hands felt so good on my body—knowing when to caress and when to squeeze. Just thinking about grinding myself against his hard length has a chill racing up my spine.

Before, it was easy to escape him and my thoughts of him. I just left work and kept myself busy with my life. But now, escaping him is impossible because not only do I work with him, but I also live with him. I have to see him in the morning at the breakfast table. I have to see him at night in his thin pajama bottoms, always noticing the outline of his manhood beneath. And even now as I sit in this uncomfortable chair with more foil on my head than can be found at any backyard barbecue, I still can't escape him. My thoughts range from everything to yelling at the bastard to watching as I slide down his length. How can one person be so perfectly right in one way and so completely wrong in another? It's beyond infuriating.

I spend the whole day at the salon/spa. The highlights they add to my auburn hair light up when they catch the sun. I get a manicure and a pedicure. I have a facial and more spa treatments than I even knew existed. And now, I'm lying on the table, prepared to have every hair yanked from my body. I've already had my face waxed of all its peach fuzz. My legs and downstairs area are next. Lord, help me.

The legs are a breeze and that part goes by pretty quickly, but when it's finished, I'm asked which style I'd like for my lady bits. I'm confused by that. I didn't realize there *were* different styles.

"What do you mean?"

"Would you like all of it gone? Or would you like to leave a patch down the center? We can do anything, dear. Hearts, stars . . . hell, even lightning bolts."

I smirk. Have my pubic hair waxed into a lightning bolt? Hell yeah! "Lightning bolt, please."

She nods and goes about her work. I have to admit, the warm wax feels nice, but then she rips it away without warning and I let out a string of curse words as my hands wrap around the edge of the table, squeezing it through the pain.

"Only a little more, dear," she insists.

Every time I think she's done, she keeps going and going and going. She's like that damn pink bunny on all those commercials. I'm about to take the wax paper out of her hand and say "enough!" but then she wipes the area with a cool, wet cloth and says, "All done." She hands over a mirror and I check it out. I smile at its awesomeness.

Now alone, I stand up in the room as my dress falls back into place. I go to put my panties on but decide against it. I need some cool air on all these hot patches under my skirt. I leave the salon and head out to get in the Uber I'd already arranged. He drives me back across town and I notice the time on the dash. Looks like I'll make it just in time for dinner. I didn't make it to the shopping part of the day since everything else took so long. I guess I'll have to go in the morning before my gym session.

I want to be mad about the gym, but the truth is, it's something I've been wanting to do for a long time. I just couldn't afford it. Living alone meant I had to pay for everything myself: rent, food, personal necessities. There wasn't a whole lot of wiggle room, and most of the time, I found myself broke by the time my next paycheck showed up. At least now I can save all that money I would've been spending. Maybe by the end of this, I'll be able to afford a better place. Or I can stay where I'm at and live in comfort for a while. I just hope I don't get too spoiled with all the gourmet meals and that deep bathtub.

I walk into his apartment and find him in the dining room, where I knew he'd be.

"Hey, how'd it go today?"

I take a seat beside him. "It went," I breathe out, making my plate of grilled chicken and salad.

"Your hair looks nice," he says, eyes drifting over my face and upper body. "Nails too."

"Thanks." I hold out my hand, looking at the nails. "I don't know how I'm supposed to do anything with these damn things on."

He chuckles. "Then why'd you get them? You could've just painted your real nails."

"I know. Just wanted to try something new," I say fanning them out and staring at them again.

"How do you like your hair?"

I shrug, indifferent. "It's fine. It's not the first time I've had highlights." I go back to eating, not wanting to talk to him since I'm still smarting over the embarrassment he caused when he rejected me.

He sets his fork down and takes a deep breath. "So you were treated well at the spa?" It's clear he's reaching for something to talk about.

I push away from the table, deciding I'm not very hungry. "Everything was great. I think I'm going to go shower. I still have sticky wax all over my body." I stand and start toward the door.

He laughs. "How was the wax? Was it as painful as you thought it'd be?"

I don't know what comes over me, but I spin around to face him. "The wax wasn't so bad. See?" I flip up my dress, flashing him a peek at the lightning bolt.

I watch as he processes what's happening. His eyes fall from mine down to the storm zone. His mouth drops open and his eyes stretch wide.

"Perfect, right?" I ask, turning and walking away—leaving him shocked. I have no idea why the hell I just did that, but I can't help the giddiness I feel as I retreat to my room to be alone. The look on his face was worth it.

I shower quickly and get out to dry. I blow-dry my hair, feeling that I have time to put in a little extra effort. Blow-drying makes it soft and it lies down perfectly, unlike what it usually does since I always just go to bed with it wet. I smother my body in a thick, heavy lotion, wanting to soothe the ache in my skin from having my hair ripped out, and I admire my lightning bolt. I think it describes me perfectly —like the storm I am. Matthew doesn't even know what he's gotten himself into. By the time I'm done with him, he's going to be paying me to get out of his house.

————

LATE SUNDAY MORNING, I wake up to find him already gone. There's no note anywhere that I can see. I eat breakfast alone, then decide I'm not up for the gym today. I'm tired from a lack of sleep last night. Every time I fell asleep, I only dreamed of how we got too close on Friday night. As if that wasn't enough torture, thinking I was going to get what I wanted only to have it ripped away was just another embarrassing reminder. I really shouldn't be surprised though.

What would a man like him see in a woman like me? We come from completely different worlds. He's handsome, charming when he wants to be, rich, and has nice things. I, on the other hand, have always been broke. I've never been able to afford nice vacations— meaning I haven't even managed to get out of the state of Illinois. He's been places, seen things. He's wise with his Harvard degree, and all I have is a degree I printed off the computer after finishing my online classes. Everything about him screams wealth and privilege while everything about me screams state-issued medical insurance and used clothing. Not that those things are bad by any means. I'm proud of myself and the way I grew up. He may have had money, but I had a family and friends who loved me. I worked hard for everything I have. And I'm a good person. Why wouldn't I be proud of myself?

Instead of going out to shop for the gym clothes I'll need then going to the gym, I decide I'll hang out in the living room watching TV, eating snacks, and repainting these nails. I don't know why I told the nail tech I was fine with the boring nude color she chose; it's not my style at all.

I go to my room and change back into my pajamas: a pair of black cloth shorts and a tank top. I gather everything I'll need for my little rest day: nail polish, remover, chips, soda, snack cakes, candy, and a couple of books. I have everything lined up on the coffee table as I sit on the couch and turn on the TV. I flip through dozens of channels, trying to find something that will keep my attention. I end up on some teen vampire movie and shrug as I drop the remote on the table. I start by taking off this plain nail polish. I do my toes first then start on my left hand. While it dries, I tear into a bag of chips. I'm sitting back on the couch with chip crumbs everywhere when he walks in.

He stops before he even sees me. "What's that smell?" He starts looking around, finding me.

"Sorry, I was bored with the polish color the lady picked out, so I decided to do them myself."

"Yourself?" he asks, face scrunching.

I hold up my hand and show him my black nails. "Much better, don't you think?"

"No, I don't think. You just ruined a $200 manicure and pedicure."

I wiggle my toes when he speaks of them.

"It's not ruined. I still have the nails on. It's just now they're a different color. A much better color. I mean, who wants nude? So boring," I mumble, shaking my head.

He grinds his teeth together, seething. "And what *is* all this shit? Aren't you supposed to be shopping and getting ready for your gym session?"

"About that . . ." I curl myself up in a ball, wanting to seem smaller. "I'm kind of tired. I didn't sleep well, so I thought I'd skip it. It's Sunday, after all. A day of rest, not a day to kill yourself."

His hands land on his hips and his jaw flexes. "You're not skipping it. I've paid a lot of money for that membership and trainer. You've already ruined a $200 manicure and pedicure, so you're not wasting any more of my money. Now clean this shit up and get off your ass!" he yells, storming off into his bedroom and slamming the door behind him.

I let out a long sigh. Oh, how I miss my quiet Sundays at home—the one day a week when I refused to leave my apartment or change out of my pajamas. I'd lounge around all day, eating and watching TV. I'd read, nap, and enjoy the silence.

I turn off the TV and start cleaning up my mess. I'm not going shopping today, but I will go to the gym. I'll go there, blow off the trainer, and instead go into their spa. Another massage couldn't hurt, especially with this now-raging headache.

TEN

MATTHEW

Well, it seems that turning her down has just brought us full circle. We're no longer playing nice—no longer on good terms. It's like she's doing everything she can to piss me off. She either ignores me completely or says things she knows will only piss me off. She ruined her nails that I just had done for a function we're attending, and now she's trying to bail on the gym? Ha! No fucking way. I'll take her myself if I have to.

I lie down in bed in an attempt to cool down. Only she can make my blood boil this way. Taking a quiet minute to myself works a little too well at relaxing me, and the next thing I know, I'm waking up. I turn my head and look over at the clock. It's going on 5 p.m., the time Poppy's supposed to be starting with her trainer. Fuck. I just know she'll be late.

I push myself up and use my private bathroom before exiting my room. To my surprise, she's no longer on the couch. The table has been cleaned and the couch is clear of crumbs. I walk down the hallway to her bedroom door and find it open and empty. Huh. Maybe she actually listened to me for once.

My cell phone rings and I pull it from my pocket. "Hello?"

"Hello, Mr. Lewis?"

"Yes?"

"Hi, this is Jake from the gym. I'm here for the training session, but I'm not finding anyone by the name of Poppy. She's still coming, isn't she?"

"Well, she isn't at home, so I assume she is."

"All right, well, just a reminder, I'm booked with her three nights a week. If she doesn't show, my rate doesn't change. It'll still cost you the same at the end of the week."

"I'm aware. Just give her a few more minutes. She's always running late."

"Will do." He hangs up the phone and I let out an annoyed breath.

Why do I have a feeling this is all part of her plan to drive me crazy? It's bad enough she wasn't up in time for brunch this morning with my family. I refuse to treat her like a child. I got tired of waiting around and left without her. Grandmother wasn't too pleased that I came alone, and Dad was surprised by the news that I had a fiancée, which prompted a long list of questions.

I decide to give her the benefit of the doubt and don't go down to the gym. I want to trust her to do as she says she will. If she doesn't, then I'll know she isn't serious about this arrangement and I'll just turn this video over to the police and be done with it all. Scaring her is the only way to get her to do anything. I find it odd how we seemed to do a 180—going from hating each other to getting along so well. Then we did another 180, putting us back where we started after I rejected her. How many more times are we going to turn in circles?

At 7 p.m., dinner is on the table and she walks in, looking calm and refreshed. She doesn't look like she's been sweating her ass off at the gym.

"Jake called," I say, capturing her attention the moment she walks into the dining room.

"Who?" she asks, wrinkling her nose.

"The trainer I hired for you. You were just there, weren't you?"

"Oh," she breathes out, already looking a little guilty. "Well, I *was* at the gym, but I didn't . . ."

"Use a trainer?" I ask.

"I didn't work out," she states.

I think I see red. "What do you mean you didn't work out? What the hell have you been doing there for the last two hours?"

"Well, I got a back massage and a foot massage. I had some cucumber water and got a facial . . ."

I cut her off. "All of those treatments cost extra. They aren't included in your membership."

"Oh, I know. I just told them to add everything to the card on file. Hope you don't mind." She offers up a smile

I have to remind myself that I can't kill her. I take a deep breath, hold it, and then slowly release it. But even that doesn't help the anger. "Let me get this straight: you ruined the manicure and pedicure I paid for, then you skipped the trainer I paid for. But you used your gym membership to get in and have more spa treatments, which I'm also paying for?"

She doesn't reply, but I see the guilt clearly written on her face.

"That's it," I breathe out, standing up so quickly that my chair nearly topples over.

"What's it?" she asks, brows drawn together.

"This is over. Get your shit and get out. I'll be turning in that video first thing in the morning and charges will be coming your way."

"What? Wait!" she says when I turn to leave the room.

My feet stop moving but I don't turn around.

"Okay, I'm sorry. I'll do what I'm supposed to do. Please don't turn in that video. I'll rot in jail. My family doesn't have the money to get me out of that kind of trouble. Please, I'll do anything," she begs.

Finally, I turn around, my mood suddenly lighter. "Anything?" I ask.

She nods. "Anything."

"You'll go to the gym and work out with your trainer?"

She nods.

"You'll go to your classes and be on time?"

Again, she nods.

"You'll continue to come to work and do your job to the best of your ability?"

She rolls her eyes but nods.

"And you'll stop with this bullshit attitude?"

"I'll do my best on that one."

I'm speechless, waiting for her to explain.

She takes a breath and says, "I just think it's probably best, in our situation, to keep our distance when we're able. Lines clearly got blurred Friday night and I don't want that to happen again. I don't want to let my guard down and fall for this *act* you're putting on. I'll do all of the things you mentioned: I'll do the family stuff and the other functions you need me for, but other than that, I'd really like to keep my distance from you for a while."

I open my mouth but am not sure how to reply. That's the exact opposite of what I want. I don't want more space between us. I want to take the space away. I want her to see the real me—not the guy she sometimes brings out in me: a rude, cocky asshole. I'd hoped that this living arrangement would force us together and something would blossom between us. But now she's pulling back? That's not what I wanted at all. However, I'm not in the mood to argue with her any further. Instead, I let her leave the room and opt to give her the space she seems to be needing. We'll readdress this in a few days after she's had time to cool off.

Over the next few days, neither of us talks more than we have to. In the mornings, we eat breakfast in silence. At work, we only talk out of necessity. After work, she goes to the gym or I do. Dinner is eaten in silence, then we go to our separate rooms. If we bump into each other around the house, nothing is said—we only exchange looks. I feel like I'm walking on eggshells in my own house. I desperately want to talk to her, but at the same time, I don't want to break first. I want her to come to me. Is that too much to ask?

It's Thursday night: day four of the silent treatment. The only sounds in the dining room are forks scraping off plates, chewing, and breathing. The silence in the room is damn near deafening. It's driving me crazy and I don't know how much longer I can take it. Once upon a time, I prayed for the silent treatment from her. But now it feels weird after seeing how we could be. I suddenly want to ask how the gym is going for her. How she's sleeping being away from home. If there's anything she needs. I don't want this to feel like a punishment, even though it technically is in her eyes.

I let out an exasperated breath and let my fork fall from my hand. It clatters against the plate loudly, getting her attention like I knew it would. "This is ridiculous, Poppy."

"What is?" she asks, still eating and looking down at her plate.

"The whole silent treatment thing. It's driving me crazy. Can't we just go back to fighting?"

The corners of her mouth begin to lift slightly, but she catches herself and pulls them back down into place. "Well, I'm sorry if I can't get along with a man who's forcing me to do things I don't want to do."

"What don't you want to do?" I ask, even though I kind of have an idea.

"I don't want to be forced into going to the gym if I'm not feeling well. I don't want to get yelled at if I don't like the color of my nails and feel like changing them. I don't want to have to argue to have basic human rights. Why is this so hard for you to understand? You don't own me." She levels her eyes on me, and even though my anger is sky-high right now, it's covered up by the longing she causes me to feel.

"Okay, look, I'm sorry for yelling at you about your nails, but I had them done that way for a reason. We have several upcoming events, and I thought plain nails would match all of your dresses."

"I didn't know we had anything to go to other than your family meals." The anger on her face begins to soften.

"I have a friend who's opening his first art gallery, and we've been invited to the grand opening. There's also a charity event my father is holding at the corporation next week. I didn't tell you because I . . . I don't know. I didn't want to give you time to come up with an excuse to miss it."

She lets out a long breath and her shoulders visibly fall. She sets down her fork and leans in toward me. "I wouldn't try getting out of our arrangement, Matthew."

"You already are," I point out. "We're supposed to be bonding and getting to know each other on a daily basis, but instead, you're completely ignoring me."

She nods. "You're right. I thought that if living with me was unbearable for you that you'd get tired of it eventually and let this whole thing go."

"Look, I know this is technically a punishment for you, but I don't want it to feel that way. I want you to enjoy being here. So can we please drop the silent treatment and go back to how we were last week?"

Her lips form a soft, shy smile and she nods. "Yeah," she agrees.

ELEVEN

POPPY

I'm thrown off guard at dinner. He really seems upset by my lack of interest in him and this game. I wanted it over, but not for the reasons he's probably thinking. I wanted it over so I'd no longer have that embarrassing reminder of how he rejected me. I wanted it over so I'd no longer have to look temptation in the eye every single day. I wanted it over so these feelings would stop in their tracks. I just wanted everything to go back to how it was: me thinking he's a sexy asshole. Seeing the human side of him has only made those feelings of attraction stronger. I didn't want it over in order to have my freedom back or anything like that, although I'm sure that's what he's assuming.

I've holed myself up in my room for four long nights now, never coming out. If I needed water, I got it from the bathroom attached to my room. Anything else could wait. But with that talk out of the way, I feel like I should start coming out again. I don't want him to think I'm still avoiding him, but I want to break the ice gently. After my shower, I decide to go to the kitchen for the chocolate cake I passed on after dinner. My hair is wet and hanging around me, soaking the back of my shirt that hangs to my knees.

I open the door and peek down the hallway, finding nothing and no sounds. I step out and walk through the living room then into the kitchen. I push through the swinging door and freeze when I'm face-to-face with him. He has the chocolate cake out of the fridge. It's sitting on the island and he's standing over it with a fork in hand, eating it directly off the cake stand.

He looks up at me with a grin—like he's been caught. "Want some?"

I giggle and nod. "Yeah," I agree, moving over to the cake on the other side of the island from him.

He opens a drawer and pulls out a fork, handing it over.

I take the fork and bend down, leaning against the island as I slide my fork through the fluffy cake. I take a bite and the sweetness overtakes me. "Mmm," I mumble with my eyes closed. I swallow it and open my eyes, finding him watching me intently.

I feel the heat creep up my cheeks. "That's really good cake," I say out of embarrassment.

He lets out a silent laugh that sounds like air quickly blowing through his nostrils, but the corners of his mouth turn up slightly. "It *is* really good." He takes another bite.

"You're going to have to hit the gym twice as hard tomorrow," I tease him.

He shrugs. "It's worth it."

I smile as I take another bite. He leans against the island in the same fashion I am, putting us almost nose-to-nose.

"Why are you staring?" I ask, feeling the heat in my cheeks only growing hotter.

He shrugs. "Your eyes are really dark tonight—like midnight: black with a hint of blue."

I swallow down the bite I just took. "Yeah, they do that sometimes. Usually it's only when—" I stop myself from talking and shove another bite into my mouth. "Never mind," I say, shaking my head and dropping my fork in the sink. "I'm going to bed."

"Wait," he says, standing up. "You're not going to leave me hanging like that, are you?"

I laugh. "Yeah, I am. Night." I push my way through the swinging door and almost run to my bedroom. I can't believe I almost admitted that my eyes only darken like that when I'm turned on. But I couldn't help it. I was standing there—watching him closely as he savored each bite. I could smell his body wash: cottonwood and musk. We were so close I could feel the heat radiating off his body and I wanted nothing more than to feel it against me again.

I push off the bedroom door I'm leaning against and get into bed. Maybe sleep will help me calm down. I can only pray.

———

I'M at the gym and hate him more than anything. I also hate myself for not staying in shape. I hate the trainer who's not cutting me any slack. But mostly, I hate that I like it. I'm sure I'm probably screwed up in the head, but something deep down is telling me to do this—to try—to see if I can become his type. I know this isn't the way to start a good relationship, but I'm not exactly trying to start a relationship either. I just want to see how differently he'll view me . . . and maybe have some fun with him along the way. If he thinks I'm suddenly his type after this *Pygmalion* makeover, he's more lost than I thought.

By the time I get back to his place, my clothes are soaked with sweat. My hair is drenched and I'm completely worn out. He's in the dining room when I come in, but I pass him by and go to shower. I wash off quickly, much too tired to spend any real time scrubbing my body. All I want to do is get clean, eat, and crash out. I pull on a T-shirt and a pair of shorts and go to the dining room to grab something quick for dinner. To my surprise, he's still sitting in the same chair.

He looks up at me when I enter. "Hey, you missed dinner, but I had them leave it out for you if you're hungry."

"Thank God. I'm starving. I would've joined you, but I think the smell coming off of me would've ruined your appetite."

He laughs. "Yeah, I've been there. How's the gym going, by the way? Are you learning to like it yet?"

I take my plate and fix a salad. "Sort of. I mean, I hate it, but I like it at the same time. It's really weird."

He nods. "I know exactly how you feel. I felt the same way when I started. But the good part is, if you don't stop, you just like it more and the hate seems to slip away."

I take a piece of grilled chicken and slice it up to top my salad.

"It looks like you're already seeing some improvements."

I look over at him to see him checking out my ass as I reach across the table for the salad dressing. I laugh. "Did you just check out my ass?"

At first, he looks like a deer in the headlights who's been caught, but that look fades away and his cocky attitude returns. "What? I'm not allowed to look at the progress I'm paying for?" He's wearing a smirk.

I shake my head clear. I feel like I should be mad, but instead, I feel almost giddy that I've gotten his attention. I don't know what that says about me, but I like it regardless. At least I don't have to explain these weird emotions to anyone, because I probably wouldn't be able to. I mean, how can a woman be so attracted to a man who's so cocky, arrogant, and downright mean at times? Yes, I'm pretty sure this speaks volumes about my character.

I take my seat and begin eating, only focusing on getting the nutrition I need so I can go to sleep. I push away all thoughts of him and how he makes me feel. It's nothing but confusing—even to me.

"I've called off dinner with my grandmother this week. I thought it might be good for us to have some alone time to regroup after our long week."

My eyes pop up to his. "What do you mean? Aren't we only doing this for your grandmother?"

He nods. "Yes, but I feel we were way off-balance and it would be worth it to take some time to ourselves. Start fresh, if you will."

I chew my food and nod. "So what's the plan?"

"You'll see," he says around a smirk as he stands.

I'm speechless as I watch him walk out of the dining room, leaving me alone.

————

"YOUR CLOTHES ARE ON YOUR BED," Matthew says when I walk in from work.

"What?"

"I mentioned that we were doing something different today, yes?"

"Yes," I reply, nodding my head once.

"Well, your clothes are on your bed." He says it slowly this time, as if I didn't understand the first time he said that same sentence.

"Okay," I mumble, heading to my room.

I drop my purse on the chair by the door and move over to the bed to see what exactly he has in store. I'm surprised when I don't find a dress and heels before me. Instead, it's a pair of white skinny jeans, some Sperry boat shoes, and a light blue polo shirt with a white sweater. That's weird. Where in the world is he taking me?

I shower and dress in the clothes that were laid out. Everything fits to perfection and I have no idea how he does it. I French-braid my hair, leaving the long braid to hang over my shoulder, and I add some moisturizer to my face, finishing it off with lip gloss and mascara. I walk out to find him waiting in the living room.

He's no longer wearing the suit he had on just moments ago. Now he's wearing a pair of khaki pants, Sperrys, and a navy blue polo. "Are you ready?"

"Yeah, I guess so," I reply.

He sets his newspaper down on the table and stands up, leading the way to the door.

On the ride, I want to ask where we're going, but I have a feeling he won't tell me anyway. So instead of driving him crazy with questions and trying to guess, I keep my mouth shut and just watch the signs on the side of the road, trying to guess where we're headed. I should be more surprised than I am when we arrive at Groveland Park. Off in the distance, I see nothing but bright, sparkling water with rows and rows of boats.

"We're going boating?" I ask, looking from the water, to him, and back.

"Yep."

Okay . . . I think, but don't say anything. I wonder what's brought on this sudden change in him—why he's suddenly more worried about me enjoying myself and not seeing our time together as a punishment. Before, he confused me because I couldn't understand why he acted the way he did, but now I'm confused because I don't understand how he can be two different people. There's the hard-edged lawyer who expects everyone to fall at his feet, and then there's this side of him. It's the side I got to see last week before our silent treatment set in—the guy he's been since he broke said treatment. He's so back and forth all the time that I feel like I may get whiplash from trying to keep up with him.

Once we're on the boat, I take a seat with a glass of champagne in hand. I'm sipping it slowly, not wanting to get a buzz, but needing to relax myself. He walks out and joins me—his own glass of something brown in hand.

"I'm sure you're probably confused," he says, looking out over the water with the sun beating down on it, "so let me explain." He finally turns to face me. "Growing up, we spent a lot of summers on the water. I wasn't here often—mostly back in Florida at my grandparents' estate there, but the sentiment is the same. You and I were on the same page when we agreed to get to know each other, but somehow, we ended up at opposite ends of the book. So this is me, taking us back to the same page—at the beginning, starting over. And I'm hoping we read at the same pace this time, instead of you jumping so far ahead."

I nod, now understanding. He wants a fresh start . . . again.

"I've rented the boat for the entire evening. It's fully staffed and they can get you anything you need. They're also preparing dinner for us as we speak. Tonight, I just want you to relax and enjoy being here. I promise I'll be on my best behavior."

I nod, taking in his words.

"I know you said you didn't want to fall for the role I was playing, so this is me not playing any role. I'm not your boss. I'm not some guy who's tricked you into spending time with him. I'm just me, Matt . . . or Matthew, as you so like to call me."

I giggle. "You don't like it when I call you Matthew?"

He glances over at me with a serious edge to his expression. "Only my grandmother calls me Matthew."

I smile wider. "Your grandmother and me. I think Matthew is much softer and kinder."

He looks over at me again with a smile. "Call me whatever you wish."

That sentence right there makes my stomach muscles tighten. In an attempt to push away the passion suddenly flooding my body, I turn it into a joke. "Can I call you Daddy?" I bat my lashes and grin.

He lets out a deep laugh. "If you wish," he agrees. "I can only imagine what the clients would think at work." His smile doesn't fade, as if he's seriously considering it.

"I think I'll stick with Matthew," I state, not even able to imagine the looks we'd get if I really did call him that.

"I think that's a good call," he agrees.

There's a long, drawn-out silence as we both watch the water and the skyscrapers we pass. I loll my head to the side, watching him and finding him more entertaining than any city scene before me. "Tell me something about your childhood. Did you like spending time on the water like this?"

He takes a sip of his drink. "I did. I preferred sailing to traveling around in a yacht. But sailing takes time to learn, and I didn't want to put either of us in danger with you being untrained. The lake can get pretty rough when the winds pick up. And salt water is more dense than fresh water. Boating here and in Florida are two completely different experiences."

"So you took sailing lessons?"

"Yes, my father thought that anyone who was anyone knew how to sail. It was mandatory in my household. I was also on the rowing team in high school. I've just always found myself drawn to the water. I'll admit, the first few lessons were pushed upon me, but I quickly fell in love with the water and the lifestyle, so every class I took from there on out was because I wanted to."

"That sounds nice. I always wanted to take lessons, but my parents couldn't afford it."

"What kind of lessons did you want?"

I snort. "Almost anything. I felt a little too ordinary, so I wanted to be different—special in any way, really. I remember begging for piano lessons, gymnastics, dance, painting . . . but I was told 'no.' That is, until I found a youth center nearby that did these things for free. I quickly found out that I suck at almost everything. I hurt myself too many times in the dance class, and I even sprained my ankle and had to go to the hospital. After that bill, my parents forced me to quit dance." I laugh. "But I enjoyed the art classes and the few piano lessons I took."

"I didn't know you could paint and play the piano."

"Oh," I laugh, "I can't. I suck at drawing and painting, but I still like to do it from time to time just to get the creative juices flowing. Piano was fun, but I only learned one song. The class was supposed to teach you the basics so you could teach yourself after learning to read music, but we didn't have a piano at home, so I never got to practice."

"Well, there's still plenty of time to learn," he says. The sun shines against his face and creates a little twinkle in his eye. I can't help but look at him in awe as I marvel at how it must feel to think everything is within reach.

TWELVE

MATTHEW

After hearing her talk about her lower-class upbringing, I know the one thing I want to do for her more than anything is get her a piano. I know the perfect place to put it too: in the living room, right in front of the floor-to-ceiling windows on the far wall. There's nothing there now other than some uncomfortable chairs I keep handy in case I have too many guests at once, but I can push them off on one of the staff members. I remember Karen liked them quite a bit when I had them brought in.

There's a music shop here in town, owned by Daniel's rock-star fiancée. I'll ask him if he could help me acquire a grand piano for her. I'll have it delivered to the house while we're at work—that way, when we come home, she'll be surprised. I'll even find someone to give her lessons. This has been my best idea yet.

Poppy and I sit on the boat deck, having a few drinks and watching the world we pass by. Around 7 p.m., dinner is served and we both go inside to have a seat at the table. The table is small—meant to be romantic by keeping us together. I've been so close to her today that I could smell her, and that only teased my senses in ways I wish it hadn't.

I feel tightly-wound, on edge, and ready to pull her against me and kiss her at any moment. I don't know how I've managed to hold it back this long; I just pray for the strength I need to keep my distance. I've only just gotten her back, and I don't want to go chasing her off yet again.

The longer I'm near her, the more I want her. And it kills me that I could've had her and I turned her down. But I keep telling myself that it was for the best. Instead of looking at her and finding everything I consider attractive about her, I focus all my energy on reminding myself why I hated her for so long. She usually talks too much. She doesn't listen—I mean, how *can* she when she does all that talking? She's lazy at work—well, at least she was before this whole arrangement started. We fight over every single thing. We come from different worlds. Everything that seems right to me is wrong to her, and everything that seems right to her is ludicrous to me. It's like her brain is the opposite of mine. I can never tell when she's being serious or when she's joking. Oftentimes, I think she's joking and she's being completely serious. When I think she's being serious, she's joking. This woman keeps me on my toes and I feel like I'm always off guard, waiting to catch the next curve ball she throws my way. As I was growing up, I learned to always be prepared, so this is more frustrating to me than anything else.

And even though I know all these things—that we couldn't possibly work out, that she has no feelings for me, and that reaching out and taking her would only end in disaster—none if it calms the longing that's swimming through my veins.

That plan clearly didn't work, so I direct my attention to the table and the food before us. There's a white tablecloth on the small, square table, and a candle in the center, the flame flickering and dancing. We each have a glass of wine and a plate filled with steak, salad, and a dinner roll. The steak is tender—slightly pink inside— and the salad is fresh and crisp. It's easy to keep my focus on the food when she's across from me trying just as hard to keep her attention off of me.

"Do you have any plans for tomorrow?" she asks, cutting through the silence like a sharp knife.

My head pops up and my eyes find hers. "No. Got something in mind?"

She smiles but tries holding it back. "Well, I don't know how you'd feel about it, but I thought that since you brought me here to show me a small part of your childhood, that I could take you to a piece of mine. What do you think?"

I let out a nervous laugh, wondering what in the world she could have in store. "Am I going to die?"

She laughs. "No, it's not dangerous at all . . . well, unless you're extremely uncoordinated. But I think you'll do fine."

"Okay," I agree, more than happy to spend more time with her— and this time, in *her* element. That might just be the key to getting her to view me differently. Here I am, trying to force her into my world. I never considered visiting hers. "What time will we be leaving?"

She shrugs a shoulder. "Around noon, I guess."

"And the attire?"

"Casual. In fact, wear the worst clothes you have. Don't want to ruin something expensive."

I don't tell her that everything I own is expensive. It would feel pointless—like rubbing it in her face or something. But I can do jeans and a T-shirt.

We finish eating and head back out on the deck to look at the night sky as we make our way back to shore. One of the staff members turns on some music, and it filters through the outdoor speakers hanging above our heads. It's a soft, slow song—something romantic, just like the dinner we had. I look over at her and hold out my hand. "Dance?"

She lets out a quiet laugh. "Okay," she agrees, setting her still-full wine glass down on the table between us.

We both stand and she slides her hand into mine. I lead her out to the center of the deck and spin her around to face me. She falls into my chest and a puff of air whooshes out of her mouth, blowing across my jaw and neck. My eyes want to close at the heat and closeness, but I hold it back as I steady her.

I start leading her around the deck with her in my arms. She's awkward at first, stiff and unsure, but the longer we dance, the looser she gets. "Let me guess, you took ballroom dancing classes as well?" she asks.

I know she's being a smart-ass, but I laugh. "I did. Does it show?"

She rolls her dark eyes. "A little."

Although it's dark outside with the sun gone, there are small lights scattered around the boat. When I spin her around, the light shines against her eyes and I see that they've dark again. Midnight with a hint of blue. I can't help but wonder what it means. When I brought it up before, she quickly changed the subject and ran off.

The last time I noticed the change in her eyes, we weren't doing anything but eating cake. She was on one side of the island while I was on the other. We were both leaning against the island, with the cake between us. We were eye-to-eye. I remember how sweet she smelled after her shower, and how beautiful she looked with her soaking-wet hair and clean skin free of all makeup. I remember how turned on I was in that moment. Then it hits me: was she turned on like I was? Does the darkening of her eyes mean she wants me? God, I wish I could test that theory. The night we got too close, were her eyes like they are now? I try thinking back, but it was so dark in the living room that night that I didn't notice . . . I couldn't notice. The fire burning in the fireplace was the only light in the room. I remember seeing it reflecting in her eyes. They were big and dark, but I couldn't see the color clearly enough.

If I leaned in right now, would she let me kiss her? Would she let me take it further? I can see myself pulling her against me and carrying her inside. I feel my body start to come to life and I push the thoughts away immediately. We're so close right now, she'd surely feel it if I got excited. That would give it all away if nothing else did. I decide not to act on anything tonight. I don't want to push her too far after I've just gotten her to talk to me again, but I will watch for this in the future—for any sign she may feel differently about me than she did before.

The song ends and she steps back. Her cheeks are burning, and her eyes are dark but sparkling. "Well, thank you for the dance, kind sir," she jokes.

"Anytime, sweetheart," I reply as I release her hand, watching her walk back to the table. She picks up her glass of wine and takes a drink. I wonder if she's using it as a way to cool off after our dance. It wasn't anything that would cause her to break a sweat, unless there were emotions bubbling to the surface she didn't want to feel.

When we make it back to the penthouse, the living room is dark, with the exception of the flames dancing in the fireplace. I have to admit, this would be the perfect setting to try for that kiss. I've never considered myself a chicken before now, but something inside me doesn't want to take the risk of losing her again, even if only for a few days. I finally have her where I want her. I have to move slowly and cautiously as if I were hunting an animal. Any sudden movements could scare her off and cause her to race away from me in the opposite direction. That's exactly what I don't want her to do. When she runs, I want her running *toward* me. Fuck, I've never had to work so hard in my life to get the girl before. But I guess that's why I'm so attracted to her. She's not easy. She doesn't just fall at my feet. She fights every step of the way, and I *like* the fight she has in her.

"Well, good night. I guess I'll see you in the morning."

She nods her head with a smile in place but doesn't reply. She stands in the same spot, watching me as I walk across the floor to my room. I step inside and turn around to close the door. I look up and she's still standing there, eyes locked on mine. Our eye contact remains until I shut the door between us. Now that I'm alone, I let out a long breath and find myself relaxing more than I have all night. Why am I wound so tightly when it comes to her? That's probably half the problem. I'm too uptight and she can feel it.

Tomorrow I'll work on controlling myself better. I'll teach myself how to be calm around her—how to relax and have fun. I've been uptight for too many years. In my world, you kind of have to be. Any sign of weakness is just another way to be torn down. Maybe I can trust Poppy enough to let my guard down.

I pull out my phone and call Foster. We haven't gone out for that drink yet, but I just need to clear my head and see what's going on in his world. We talk about work and I eventually fill him in on Poppy— just that she's my assistant and we've started something up. I can hear a tinge of disappointment in his voice when I ask him how things are going with his father and the Bianca situation. He never talks about how it's not the life he wants, but I know him. He doesn't want an arranged marriage or the life his family has set up for him. A few months back, we got a little too drunk at poker night and he let it slip that he wants to be able to find love on his terms—to date a woman knowing there's potential for a real future and that he's not wasting her time until he has to marry Bianca.

After our call, I take a shower and go to bed, staying in my room for the rest of the evening. When I wake in the morning, I feel ready to start the day. I'm well-rested and excited to see what she has in store for us. I dress as she advised in jeans and a T-shirt, and leave my room to find her already at the breakfast table. She's wearing a pair of tight skinny jeans. They're dark-washed and hug every curve. She's wearing a pair of combat boots, laced tight. Her hair is in a ponytail and she's wearing a black tank top that ends just above her belly button, showing me a small sliver of her tight and toned stomach.

"Good morning," I say, walking into the room. "You look like you're going to war," I joke.

She smiles and looks at me from beneath her long, dark lashes. "I am. Eat up. You'll need your strength."

I laugh but take my seat, preparing to fix my plate. She sits down beside me and picks up a slice of bacon, putting it in her mouth and chewing slowly.

This is a first. I haven't seen her eat bacon since she started her gym regimen. She's been sticking to fruit, yogurt, and oatmeal.

She shrugs at my expression. "I need the protein if I'm going to take you to my old stomping grounds."

I laugh. "Where are we going? *The Hunger Games?*" I joke, wondering if I need to break out a bulletproof vest.

She rolls her eyes. "No, but this could be considered just as dangerous."

"You said I wouldn't die," I remind her.

She laughs. "You'll be with me. You'll be fine," she promises.

THIRTEEN
POPPY

Matthew has no idea what I have in store for him, and I can see how much that's getting to him. His back is stiff, he's jittery, and doesn't seem to be able to hold a conversation as I drive. He likes to be in control of everything. Today isn't just about giving him a glimpse of my childhood—it's also about getting him to relinquish some of that control he feels he always needs to have. I have to admit, though, the boating trip last night was nice.

Everything about last night was nice. Conversation flowed easily between the two of us. I felt like we made a real connection and I was surprised to see the real him. I'd always thought the side of him I saw at work was the real him, but last night showed me that wasn't the case. I saw past his control issues, insecurities, and cocky exterior. I saw his life through his eyes. I saw what made him the way he is—the way he thinks he has to be. I saw past all of that and saw a good man with a kind heart . . . he just needs to be coaxed out a bit.

The weather last night was beautiful. It was a cloudless night with a sky full of stars and a big, bright moon. There was a soft breeze, but not enough to make you cold—just enough to keep you cool. The water was smooth, allowing for an easy drift. And then there was Matthew in a relaxed mood. When his arms enveloped me and he pulled me against his chest as we danced, it was like he sucked the air from my lungs. I was left breathless. When our eyes locked, my heart skipped a beat and my whole body flooded with need. I'm sure it showed in my eyes, and I'm thankful he didn't notice.

But now, here we are on our way to a blast from my past. We make the drive out of the city to Rowdy Ronnie's Extreme Sports. The sign is big, with the letters written in white and covered with paintball splotches.

He looks over at me, confused. "This is where we're going?"

"Mm-hmm, they have the best course for paintball," I say, parking the car.

"Paintball? We're shooting each other with paintball guns?" I'm not sure if he's upset by this or excited.

"That's right. I used to spend every weekend here. I'm a bit of a local legend." I flash him a smile.

He laughs but doesn't seem to believe me—that is, until we walk in and the owner, Ronnie, greets me with open arms. "Ah, the prodigal daughter returns!" He pulls me in for a hug and I can't help but laugh.

I pull back. "Ronnie, this is Matthew."

"Matt," he corrects, shaking his hand.

"Well, it's nice to meet you, Matt. You must be special to this one here if she's bringing you around. She's never brought anyone here."

I roll my eyes. "That's because I knew if I brought any of my boyfriends here and kicked their ass at paintball, they'd break up with me. This has always been my little secret. The only people who know I come here are the ones who *already* come here."

Ronnie looks down at me proudly. "Well, you'll have your work cut out for you today. There's a new gang running the ship."

I look up, all playfulness now gone. "Who are they?" I rush around the counter to view the monitors.

"Oh, they're harmless. They're just a group of high school boys, but they've been battling it out with everyone else in the hope of replacing your picture on the wall. I hope you've been practicing."

I snort as I examine the screens. "I don't need practice. I'm naturally talented. Let's get going, Matthew. We have a war to win," I tell him, grabbing the things Ronnie lets me keep under the counter. I grab my gun and start loading it full of paintballs. Next, I wrap my bandana around my head, making sure I keep my hair out of my face so it won't distract me. I pull my goggles over my eyes and look at Matthew, who's still standing there, looking at me with a dumb expression, like he has no idea what world he's stepped into.

He's smirking a bit—like he can't believe what he's seeing. "Are you serious?" he asks as Ronnie starts handing him gear.

"Like a heart attack. I can't let those kids take my title. I'm the queen around here."

He pulls his goggles over his eyes. "You know, queens usually have armies that handle the fighting for her, plus evil henchmen to do her bidding."

"Not this queen. This queen isn't afraid to get her hands dirty. Locked and loaded?" I ask.

He looks down at his gun. "I guess. I don't even know how to work this thing," he says, turning it in all different directions.

I let out a long breath. Of course he doesn't. His prissy ass probably never got to do this shit growing up. He was too busy sailing yachts and taking golf lessons. I give him a quick rundown on how to operate the gun, then before we push through the door, I tell him the rules.

"Okay, look, there are already six people out there. Four of them are together. So we'll take out the team of two, then we'll cover each other to take out the larger team. If you get hit in the kill zone, you're done and you have to leave the course. So aim for the chest or stomach, got it? Don't fuck around with an arm or a leg. Let's go!"

I push through the door and enter the course. I dart to my right, where I know there's a trail all the way around the course. The course is mostly constructed of wood, with different areas cut out so you can snake through them or shoot out of them. It's basically a big maze. There are many ways in and out, but all eventually lead to the center. Once you're in the center, you're trapped.

I could tell from watching the monitors that the big team of four likes to keep closer to the center, sending out a guard or two at a time to do a sweep. The team of two was doing what I'm doing now—snaking around the course hoping to finding someone unguarded. There's a 90-degree angle up ahead. Someone in a hurry rushes around the corner. By the time he sees me, I've already shot off three paintballs—all of them hitting him in the gut.

"Damn it," he breathes out, looking at the neon pink paint. I'm the only one who has pink paint. The rest are red, blue, yellow, and green. Ronnie keeps it that way for teams. But I'm the queen and pink is my color. Everyone who walks out of here in pink knows they've been taken down by the queen.

After checking the color of paint on his shirt, he looks up in awe. "You're her, aren't you?" he asks, eyes wide with disbelief.

I give him a quick nod with a smirk as I pass him by, leaving him behind us.

"I guess you weren't joking about being famous here, huh?" Matthew says from behind me.

"Shh, you'll give away our location," I whisper-yell back to him.

"You take this way too seriously, you know that?" he replies.

I stop and turn around. "This *is* serious! This is my reputation we're protecting. Keep it down or I'll take you out myself."

He smirks. "What if I take you out?"

"You wouldn't dare," I threaten, giving him the most serious look I can muster.

His grin doesn't fade but he shrugs one shoulder.

I turn back around and make my way to the left, taking another trail around to the center.

"So, can people climb in here? Do I need to be looking up?"

"Some do since it's not considered illegal, so just be aware," I tell him, pushing on. When I round another corner, I catch a glimpse out of the corner of my eye. Someone is following us. I get to the end of the path and drop down on my belly, pushing Matthew back behind the next corner. The guy comes around the corner quickly, but he doesn't look down. I take my shot and it hits him square in the chest.

"Fuck," he says, not really seeming to care. He looks down at me as I'm getting to my feet. "You're better than I thought you'd be."

I send him a flirty smile. "Don't underestimate the queen. Buh-bye." I wave sweetly before rushing past Matthew to lead the way.

We're getting closer to the center now, and I can hear the boys. They're just hanging out and talking, thinking they're hot shit because they haven't been taken out yet.

"It's time for the next round. There are only two people left out there. Find them," the leader says.

I hear the heavy footsteps of the two guys being sent out. I lean closer to Matthew. "Go after them," I whisper.

"And leave you here to take out the leader? Not a chance."

Ugh. "I don't need your protection right now."

"No, but I need yours," he argues.

I roll my eyes and shake my head, but lead us forward. I skip over the path that leads to the center, wanting to go after the two roaming guys first so there won't be any surprises later. As I turn the first corner, I see just a leg as one of them steps back behind a wall. I don't know if he kept moving or if he's waiting, knowing that we're on his trail, so I proceed with caution. I pause momentarily, listening for retreating footsteps, but there's nothing. It's so quiet I can still hear the other two in the center. He's waiting for us.

I know if I step around that corner, he'll fire. Even if I'm low, he'll hit Matthew in the chest and he'll be out. I need to figure out a way to keep him safe. There's a small circular cutout halfway up the wall. "Boost me up," I whisper so quietly I'm not even sure if he can hear me, but he must have, because he releases his gun, letting it hang over his shoulder as he picks me up. I grab the small hole and heave myself up higher, able to grab the top of the wall. I stick my foot in the hole, pushing myself up to the top, then shimmy my way over to the corner.

I motion for Matthew to shoot and he does, his paintball hitting the wall. It makes the kid I'm watching from above jump, and when he jumps, he steps away from the wall slightly, giving me just enough room to shoot him in the back. He spins around, surprised, but he doesn't know where the shot came from. He looks both ways, spinning in a circle. Finally, he looks up and I shoot him in the chest.

"Dammit," he breathes out, wiping his hand over the pink paint.

"Leave now and warn no one," I tell him, hopping down from the wall that's roughly seven feet high.

Matthew walks around the corner just as the kid is leaving. "That was awesome!"

"Shh, we still have three more."

Almost on cue, another one comes around the corner to complete his rounds. Matthew is quick and spins around, firing off a shot. It lands perfectly in the center of the kid's stomach.

"Yes! Did you see that?" he cheers himself on.

I smile wide, suddenly filled with pride. "I did. Good job!" I high-five him and we both stand, watching the kid retreat.

We make our way back to the center and I hear the two remaining kids. "They've been gone a while. Should we go check on them?"

There's a long pause while the other kid considers this. "Yeah, I guess so. You go left and I go right?" I hear one of them say.

I quickly dart forward and round the corner, waving for Matthew to step back around the other. He does so and I know we've got them.

"All right. Let's go. We need to finish up. I've got homework tonight," the other says.

Moments later, he rounds the corner and I let off a shot. But so does he. We're both quick, but I'm a better shot, because mine hits his stomach while his grazed my arm. At almost the same time, I hear two more shots being fired. The kid and I rush around to see who was hit. His teammate turns to face us, and he has a big blue paint splat on his chest, right over his heart.

"He got me, man," the kid whines.

"She got me too," the other kid adds on.

"And that, boys, is why your picture won't be on my wall," I say, skipping past them and grabbing Matthew's hand as I pass.

The two of us walk back into the little shop, where Ronnie's been watching everything. The moment we do, Ronnie comes rushing over to us. "That was awesome, Poppy! God, I've missed you around here." He hugs me closely.

I hug him back. "Well, my teammate came through." I pull away and turn back to look at Matthew, who's standing there looking just as proud as I feel.

"I have a few people who would like a picture with you if you have time."

I smile up at Matthew. "Of course I have time for pictures," I say. "But no autographs," I add on, sounding much more serious.

Ronnie laughs. "All right. Come on, boys!" he calls to them. They walk out from the changing rooms, now out of their gear.

"That was so awesome!" one says.

"You really are a badass," another adds on as we all line up for a picture.

Ronnie snaps it and hands the phone over to the guys.

"Nice playing with you, boys, but never forget who the queen is." I smile and wave as they walk out.

FOURTEEN

MATTHEW

Watching her dominate the paintball match was like watching an action movie starring Scarlett Johansson. I wouldn't have been surprised if she'd been shooting at people mid-cartwheel. She was amazing to watch and I'm glad I didn't drag her down. I actually shot a couple of people and made her proud. I can see it when I look into her eyes, which seem to be growing darker.

On our walk back to the car, I bump her shoulder with mine. "You were really good in there."

She smirks. "Thanks. You weren't so bad yourself."

"Nah, I'm nothing compared to you. You really have your strategy down. Remind me to be on your side if a zombie apocalypse or the purge ever breaks out. I have a feeling you'd be prepared."

She laughs. "Only if the weapons being used are paintball guns. I know nothing when it comes to real guns."

This time, I climb behind the wheel and she takes the passenger seat. "That was really fun," I tell her, starting the car and pulling my seatbelt across my chest. "What else did you do growing up?"

She shrugs. "Lots of stuff. Skating, camping, muddin'."

"What's mudding?"

She looks over at me in surprise. "You've never been muddin'?"

I laugh. "Sorry, *muddin'*. And nope, I guess not. What is it?"

"It's where you go out in the woods on a four-wheeler. You ride trails, go through mud holes . . . essentially just play in the mud." She shrugs.

"I've never even been on an ATV."

"What?" She seems really surprised, if not offended.

"I'm sorry. I was a prissy boy. I wasn't allowed to get dirty."

"Well, we'll have to fix that."

"You can show me how to drive one of those things?"

"Yeah, it's easy," she says, waving her hand through the air.

"It's a date then. I'll arrange to get us some ATVs and you'll teach me."

She smiles. "I'll be there," she promises, not contesting the fact that I called it a date.

I drive us back to the apartment and we both go to our rooms to shower. When we emerge, we're both fresh and clean and our clothes have already been laundered.

"Hey, want to go out for dinner tonight?" I ask, sick of being in the house.

"Sure, what'd you have in mind?"

I shrug. "What are you in the mood for?"

"Hmm," she mumbles, thinking it over. "Honestly, I'm kind of beat from running around all day. Why don't we order a pizza, put our pajamas on, and find a movie? Date night in?" She raises an eyebrow.

The moment I hear *date night*, I can't turn it down. "All right," I reply, grabbing my phone from my pocket. "Any requests for pizza toppings?"

"Everything. Oh, and some breadsticks too. I'm going to go change." She rushes out of the room and I Google local pizza places since I never order delivery. I call the first one on the list with the best reviews and place my order: one large pizza with almost everything and an order of breadsticks. After the call is placed, I go to my room to change out of my jeans and sweater.

I pull on a pair of silk pajama bottoms and a black T-shirt. I slip my feet into my house shoes and walk back into the living room to find her on the couch, remote in hand. I freeze, and that makes her freeze.

"Did you want to pick the movie?" she asks, probably thinking that's why I'm frozen in place, but it has nothing to do with the movie. I'm frozen because she picked the shortest shorts known to man. In fact, they may not be shorts at all. They're more like boyshort underwear. On top, she's wearing a black tank top that ends above her belly button. The straps over her shoulders look so thin that I'm pretty sure I could break them simply by touching them. And she isn't wearing a bra. I can see the hardness of her nipples through the thin cotton shirt.

I flex my jaw and push myself forward. "No, go ahead," I tell her, taking my seat on the couch at her side and grabbing a pillow to put over my lap so she doesn't see how excited I am to be this close to her. Jesus, I feel like I'm in middle school.

She settles on some horror movie and I'm secretly hoping she gets scared. I can see her leaping into my arms, our eyes connecting and drawing us closer . . . finally leading to that kiss I've been thinking about nonstop. I'm sure if this were a movie, that's probably how it would play out. But after seeing her take on all those kids today by herself, I'm sure she isn't afraid of anything. We're only about 20 minutes into the movie when the doorbell rings. I go to retrieve the pizza. I slip him some cash and go back to the couch, setting the food on the coffee table in front of us. She gets up and grabs some water, plates, and napkins. We both dig in while keeping our attention on the movie.

I find myself watching her more than the actual movie though. I can't help myself. She's far more interesting than any movie on TV. I find it cute how she watches so wide-eyed, like she can't tear her eyes from the screen. When the music gets quiet and the screen goes dark, she worries her bottom lip. When the killer jumps out, she grabs a blanket off the back of the couch and uses it as a shield. It's draped over her body, but she holds the edge up closer to her face, hiding her emotions.

"Are you scared?" I lean in and whisper.

"No," she replies quickly. "Yes," she admits soon after.

"Want to hold my hand?" I ask in a teasing tone. I hold it up, but she scoots her body up, wedging herself between the back of the couch and my side. She rests her head on my shoulder and holds the blanket just below her eyes. Her heat sinks into me and warms me in ways I didn't know I could be warmed. She smells sweet and delicious, nearly making my mouth water thinking about actually being able to taste her. Her breathing picks up and I turn to look at her. Her eyes meet mine and I can see the fear and excitement in them. I lose myself in her eyes, unable to tell if they're darkening due to the darkness in the room or something else.

Without thinking, I close the distance between us. My lips find hers and she sucks in a loud breath. All too quickly, she pushes me away.

"What are you doing?" she asks, shocked.

I let out a long breath, annoyed with myself. "I just thought . . ." I'm unable to finish.

"Well, you thought wrong!" She stands up and starts pacing in front of me. "We can't let this happen. This isn't real, remember?" She motions between us.

I'm suddenly too annoyed, so I stand up as well, with the coffee table between us. "I'm sorry. It just seemed like you were into me."

"And how did you draw that conclusion?" It's easy to tell by her tone of voice that she's mad—but whether mad at me or herself, I don't know.

"*How?*" I yell. "We danced last night and you didn't act like you didn't want me to touch you. Then today, we had a great day—we had fun together. Then when we got home, you suggested staying home, and then you put on that." I motion toward her body.

She looks down at herself then back up at me. "Are you saying that because I dressed like this, it's the only excuse you needed to kiss me? That I was asking for it?"

I roll my eyes. "Fuck, Poppy. I thought you were into me and giving me hints. I mean, what else is that outfit supposed to mean?"

"It's not an outfit. I'm wearing pajamas, and it means I'm not used to living with anyone else and it's all I have to sleep in. God . . ." Her hands move up to tangle in her hair.

"Then what's with your eyes? Huh? The closer we've been getting lately, the darker they've been."

"They're my eyes! I don't control their color."

"I thought the color change meant you were . . . turned on or something," I let the words fall from my mouth in a hushed tone.

She laughs.

"Look, if I have it all wrong, I'm sorry. But you have to admit you've been throwing me some pretty strong signals."

"What signals?" she yells.

"Are you saying you don't want me to kiss you?" I ask, stepping around the table. "Because if you tell me you don't want me to kiss you, I won't do it ever again. Is that what you want?" I ask, walking closer.

"This thing we're doing is confusing our bodies. I don't want us getting lost in that," she says, but I didn't hear an answer in that.

"Do you want me to kiss you? Yes or no?" I ask again.

"Matthew, this shouldn't happen." Again with the deflecting.

I step up to her and level my eyes on hers. They're dark again with a hint of blue. "Yes or no?" I ask deeply, slowly.

Her eyes stay locked on mine and her shoulders fall as she breathes out. "Yes."

That's all I needed to hear. My arms wrap around her. I place one on her lower back, pulling her chest to mine. The other is on the back of her head, tangling in her hair and bringing her lips right where I need them. When our lips touch, it's like a fire igniting—a flash burn. The heat consumes my lips then my face before quickly moving throughout my entire body. Her lips part and my tongue slides inside her mouth. When it brushes against hers, I pick her up against me and she wraps her arms around my neck and her legs around my hips.

I step forward, pressing her against the wall so my hands are finally free to roam her body. I squeeze her ass, her hips, her thighs. All the while, our kiss never breaks; it only gains intensity. Her fingers thread into my hair, gently tugging against the roots as she nips my lower lip. I can feel the pinch between her teeth, but there's no pain. All I can think about is sliding into her, owning her.

I'm not sure how far she'll let this go, though, so I want to take it slow and give her the time she needs to process what we're doing, and what it could mean for us. Her arms fall from my neck, but I find them quickly pushing my shirt up my stomach and chest. I remove my hands from her for a moment—only long enough to rip the shirt over my head. Our kiss breaks, but the moment the shirt's off, she moves right back in. She kisses me hard and fast, like she's starving for air and I'm the only source.

I kiss across her cheek, down to her jaw, and to her neck while my hands push up her little tank top. Apparently, I'm moving too slowly for her, so she reaches for it herself, tearing it up over her head and exposing her bouncing breasts to me. Fuck, they're perfect. They're full and round—the perfect handful. The skin of her breasts is slightly lighter than her neck and arms, which tells me she likes to get a lot of sun. The tan line is sexy as fuck, though, and I can't help but stare at them, frozen. Her nipples are tiny, hard, and the perfect rose color that reminds me of raspberries.

I move my lips to her collarbone, slowly making my way toward her exposed chest. As I kiss the swell of her breasts, my hands move up to cup and caress them. I kiss lower and lower until I can suck a hard nipple into my mouth. When I flick my tongue against her, she lets out a whimper that drives me mad.

She doesn't ask me to, but I quickly pull her away from the wall and carry her into my room. We collapse onto the mattress, still tangled up in each other. I kiss lower, to her toned stomach, then to her hips, where her shorts get in the way. Pulling my knees up underneath me, I begin tugging on the material, slowly yanking them down her hips. I don't stop until they're completely off, getting tossed on the floor.

I pick up her knee and press a kiss to the inside, kissing my way up to the junction between her parted legs. I move to the other knee, starting the process all over again. This time, when I get to her core, I slide my fingers into the waistband of her panties and push them down. She's finally fully exposed to me and I want to laugh at her lightning bolt, but I don't. The only thing I can think about is tasting her—finding out if she's as sweet as I've been imagining.

"Beautiful," I whisper, taking her in.

I move my mouth to her center, running my tongue between her folds, and her sweetness hits me like I've just bitten into a luscious peach. When I flick my tongue against her clit, her hands turn into fists, the sheet balled up in them. She lets out a soft whimper, and her knees—which are on either side of my head—begin to tremble.

If I'm honest, pleasuring a woman orally has never been my favorite part of a sexual experience, but watching her melt under my touch is driving me wild. These months of watching her, waiting for her, and wanting her, have only let me imagine this moment and the things I'd do to her given the chance. And I plan on checking off every damn item on my list tonight.

As my mouth works her over, her breathing gets harder and louder. Her legs shake more violently and her back begins to arch upward. I hold her hips down where I need them and push her over the edge, enjoying every minute I have her honeyed sweetness on my tongue.

When she goes limp beneath me, I remove myself from her, kissing my way back up her body as I work to free myself from my pajama bottoms. I'm on my knees, hovering over her, pushing my pants down my hips, but she places her hands on my chest and pushes me back. I lose my balance and topple over. I'm surprised and caught off guard, wondering if she's finally seen the light. Did I finally push her too far? Is she going to run away from me now? But instead of getting up and running away from me, she moves between my legs. Perched on her knees before me, her dark eyes lock on mine. I haven't lost her yet.

FIFTEEN

POPPY

I don't know what I'm doing, but I don't give myself a second to think about it. I don't want to think about how this could complicate things for us tomorrow, or how this could affect the rest of the agreement we have in place. But deep down, I don't care. I've seen more of the real Matthew than ever before. He's bared his soul to me without even realizing it, and because of that, I see the man he is, and I need him more than ever.

He seems surprised when I push him away from me. He's wearing a panicked expression like he doesn't know if I'm about to run off or break down and cry. But neither is the case. I've dreamed of this day for so long now that there's no way I'm not getting what I want. And what I want is to feel him beneath me. I want to know how soft his skin is, how hard he can get, and what he tastes like. I reach out and wrap my hand around his massive length, slowly moving it up and down.

He lets out a hushed breath and his head falls back against the pillows. He doesn't seem to be in any hurry. Like me, he just looks to be enjoying something he's thought about for so long now. I don't give myself time to think about that, considering I thought he hated me most days. I lean forward, sliding his tip into my mouth. I swirl my tongue around it and his head pops up to watch me. I feel his muscles begin to harden—his thighs beneath my arms, and the stomach muscles I can see when I look up.

Slowly, I take him deeper and deeper, all the way to the back of my throat. I suck and swirl and repeat the process, bobbing my head along his length. His breathing picks up and his hand flies to the back of my head, fingers tangling into my hair. He tugs slightly but not painfully. It's just the hardened edge I need. His hips start to lift with my movements, like he can't bear the thought of me removing myself from him. His breathing gets louder as his lips part, and even though his head is still up, his eyes are closed, blinded by too much passion to watch me.

"Oh, fuck. You have to stop," he says in a pleading tone. "Stop or I'm going to cum in that pretty mouth of yours." His tone is one of a weak man, like he's hanging on for dear life and suddenly asking for forgiveness for all of his past sins.

I keep going, yearning to taste him on my tongue. "Fuck, Poppy," he breathes out, his head finally falling back against the pillows. He lets out a moan that has my stomach muscles tightening, and soon after, he's spilling himself. Hot ribbons fill my mouth, and I swallow them down as I continue to work for more. His hips are suddenly mad and have a mind of their own as they lift and fall and become erratic. I take every gush he gives me, not pulling away until there's nothing left.

When I pull away, I wipe my mouth as I look up at him. His chest is rising and falling quickly and his eyes are closed so tightly that wrinkles and creases are forming around them. While he recovers, I bend down, kissing the hard muscles of his six-pack, working my way up. By the time I reach his chest, he's hard again. I lean over and open his bedside drawer. My assumptions are correct and I grab a condom. I tear it open and slide it down him. Finally, I climb on top of him and his hands find my hips as I position myself right where I need to be.

Without warning, his hands pull me down and his cock slides into my wetness, connecting us as one. We both let out a sound of relief at finally being welded together. I go to lift myself up, but he holds me down. "Hold on," he whispers, trying to get control of himself.

I'm wound so tightly that my muscles begin to tighten and release around him. The hold he has on my hips begins to lighten and I start slowly moving up and down.

"You're so fucking amazing," he breathes out, bringing his lips back to mine. Adding the kiss to the sensations already flooding my body has my hips moving more quickly. One hand leaves my hip to cup my breast, where he massages and kneads it, his thumb grazing back and forth over my hardened nipple.

I feel my release building as I grind against him, his pubic hair adding sensation to my needy clit. I moan into his mouth and his hands are back on my hips, tightening as they move me faster. My release builds high and shatters, raining down on me like hot lava— thick, fast, and unrelenting. I ride out every last wave of pleasure, and just as I collapse, he rolls us over and picks up the slack.

My legs open wide, giving him the room he needs to thrust into me as hard as he can. Every single one of his muscles is tight and hard, rippling with his movements. He pushes forward and the head- board bangs off the wall with a loud thud, but that doesn't stop him from doing it again and again. His thrusts become harder, pushing me up the bed with each one, and even though his size is enough to cause pain, the added pressure mixes with my release and creates a deli- cious cocktail, and I'm suddenly parched, ready to consume it.

"You're so fucking perfect," he breathes out, not missing a beat. It only takes a few more minutes before we're both completely lost in each other.

———

MY EYES FLUTTER open in the morning and I look around the room. I see a dark wooden bedside table, the entrance to a bathroom that doesn't look familiar, and a pressed suit hanging on the closet door. This isn't my room. I try to move but feel stiff and sore. That's when the night before comes flooding back to me. I remember every touch, every kiss, every heavy breath. I remember the sensations that flooded my body—the blinding passion and need. Everything was amazing in that moment, but how will today go?

Will he pretend that nothing happened? Will our arrangement be over now that he's gotten what I didn't even know he wanted? Will this be some kind of turning point for our relationship? I don't know and I'm suddenly nervous, waiting to find out. I roll to my back and look up at the white ceiling. I turn my head to the side and see his sleeping form: his thick, dark hair, his strong, muscular back, the top of his toned ass before the sheet cuts it off from my view.

I roll to my side to face his back, and something inside me is begging for more. I want to run my fingertips down his spine and move over to those little dimples on either side of it. I want to scoot closer and press my naked chest to his bare back, then wrap my arm around his waist and let it fall beneath the sheet to see how excited he is to be waking up. I want him to roll into my touch, onto his back with his sleepy smile in place. I want to climb on top of him again and relive last night and make sure it wasn't a dream.

The stiffness in my body tells me it wasn't a dream, but it was so perfect that it must have been. Everything about last night is what dreams are made of. The way he touched me, the way he seemed to sense what I needed before I had to ask, the way he kissed me full of passion and need and want. I want to hear all of the words he said: "perfect, amazing, beautiful."

My skin flushes when I think about last night. It burns with need again. I scoot myself to his back and wrap my arm around his waist, my hand finding his silky-soft cock. I wrap my hand around it, slowly moving it up and down. He lets out a sleepy moan and his breathing picks up, no longer deep and rhythmic. He rolls to his back and his dark eyes open. They find mine and the corners of his mouth turn up slightly. Instead of saying anything, he just pulls my mouth to his and allows me to take my place on top of him. His hands tour my body— touching my breasts and hips, then running a finger between my folds to spread my wetness. He knows exactly when I need a firm grab and a soft caress, and before I know it, he's filling me again. This time, it's much slower, more teasing.

He sits up and wraps one arm around my waist, lifting me up and dropping me down again while his mouth never leaves mine. I wrap my arms around his neck and kiss him like he's the air I need to breathe. His dark hair is a mess from my hands running through it, and he has a dark shadow on his angular jaw. His hooded eyes are filled with lust, and just looking at him has me ready to fall apart again. It doesn't take long before we're both falling over the edge together.

We both collapse back onto the bed and he has an arm under my head, keeping me close to his side. Our breathing is hard as we try to regain control of our bodies. Suddenly, he lifts his head and looks at the clock on the table.

"Shit," he breathes out.

"What's wrong?" I ask, not ready to part just yet.

"Brunch."

———

"SO YOUR DAD'S going to be there?" I ask as we're in the car, driving over to his grandmother's house.

He nods. "Yep, good ol' dad himself."

"Sound I be worried? Is he going to hate me?"

He shrugs. "He hates everyone . . . even me. So don't let it bother you." He turns into the gated driveway and puts in the code. The gates open and he hits the gas.

We're greeted in much the same fashion as we were the last time

I was here, then led into the lounge area. His grandmother is already sitting with a champagne flute in hand.

"Good morning. Please sit and have a drink with me."

Matthew bends down and takes two flutes, handing one off to me as we take our seats.

I look down at my glass, suddenly wondering what's inside. It looks to be orange juice. I guess rich people have to make every ordinary thing look fancy. I lift it to my lips and take a sip. I don't know what else is in there, but it's delicious. Maybe just some sparkling water? Maybe another kind of juice?

"How was your weekend?" his grandmother asks him.

He nods. "Very good. We went out on Lake Michigan on a yacht. We had dinner and danced."

"And then we went paintballing," I add on, but suddenly have no idea why.

Her face blanches. "Paintballing? What on earth?"

I shouldn't have said anything, but now I feel as if I need to explain. "It's where you go through an obstacle course, shooting each other with little balls of paint."

She lets out a laugh. "Oh, be serious. You're a funny one, aren't you?"

She thinks I'm joking? I don't have a chance to ask, because someone else is walking into the room. Based on how everything suddenly feels strained, I bet it's Matthew's father.

Matthew stands and shakes his head. "Dad, this is my fiancée, Poppy." He looks at me and I quickly stand up as he continues. "Poppy, this is my father, Matthew Lewis II."

The name makes me want to laugh. Of course he's Matthew Lewis II. I push back my laughter and shake his hand. "It's nice to finally meet you, sir. Matthew has told me so many wonderful things about you."

He laughs one bitter-sounding laugh. "I doubt that." He quickly turns away. "Mother, how are you doing this morning?" he asks, bending down to kiss the top of her head.

"A little tired. This medication has me sleeping my days away, but other than that . . ."

"Brunch is served, ma'am," the maid says.

We all stand and follow along behind her to the outside patio. Walking into the backyard is nothing short of amazing. The garden is beautiful and perfectly manicured with bright flowers and designer-looking trees. The patio is paved brick with fountains and statues. And there's a long patio table covered in expensive-looking dishes, silverware, and drinkware designed by Martha Stewart herself. In the center of the table is a beautiful bouquet of flowers, surrounded by platters of food—far more than we could ever eat. I wonder what she does with the leftovers, but feel it's not appropriate to ask.

"So . . . fiancée, huh?" his father asks as he takes the napkin off his plate and flings it out. "When did that happen?"

"A few weeks ago," Matthew answers.

"Where's the Audi R8, and why in the world are you driving that Corvette?"

Matthew's eyes glide to me and he smirks but wipes it away. "Oh, it got damaged in the parking lot at work. It should be fixed soon."

"See, that's another reason you need to come and work for me."

"I thought we'd talked about this, Dad. There's more than one reason why I live the way I do. I think it's time you accepted it."

His dad laughs. "Oh, I'll never accept it. My only son wants to go out and live like there isn't a family empire to run? It's ludicrous."

"All right, Dad. Can we please just have one nice meal together? For Poppy's sake?"

He scoffs. "For Poppy's sake." His eyes glance toward me. "No offense, honey, but I know my son, and you won't be walking down the aisle. Not with him at least." He looks back at Matthew, mouth open and ready to continue, but Matthew cuts him off.

"Are you fucking serious? Are we really doing this shit again?" He stands up. "You can. I'm done." He holds out his hand for me and I graciously accept it.

"Poppy, dear," his grandmother calls from behind us, and we both stop and spin around. "If it isn't too much to ask, I would like to take you to tea time next Sunday instead of dealing with these ridiculous children. This is the second time I've met you and I still haven't gotten to speak with you directly."

I force a smile and nod. "I'd love that," I agree.

Matthew turns us around and we enter the house, stride through it, and walk back out the front door. The whole way, his jaw is flexed and he's seething. But I don't push him to talk to me. If my father said something like that, I wouldn't be happy either. How disrespectful! No wonder Matthew acted the way he did.

He opens my door and allows me to slide inside—still a gentleman even though he's angry. He closes it and walks around, taking his place behind the wheel. The engine starts and he revs it loudly before shifting into gear and taking off. I have to hold on for dear life given the way he's driving, but I hold my tongue, not wanting to add to his discomfort. When we get to the apartment, he goes straight into his office and shuts the door behind him, leaving me alone and wondering what to do.

SIXTEEN

MATTHEW

I can't believe my father. How could he say something like that to her? I mean, sure, we're not really getting married, but *he* doesn't know that. For all he knows, we're really engaged, and for him to say I'd never follow through tells me exactly what my father really thinks of me. I don't know how to explain this to her, so I don't even try. Not yet, anyway. Right now, my first and only thought is to calm down. I don't want to go out there angry. I might fuck up and take this out on her, and now isn't the time for that. Not after how we spent our night and morning. We haven't even been able to address that yet.

What does this even mean to her? What does it mean to me? I guess we could both go with the obvious excuse and say it was nothing but a moment of passion—that we'd both been wound too tight and were in the right place at the right time. But I know that isn't the case on my end. However, being with her—*actually* being with her—was way more than I'd expected. When I thought about how she would be, feel, and taste, I never imagined it would be *this* good. I feel like I've had my first hit, and already, I'm addicted.

Even as I sit here right now, alone in my office with a strong drink in my hand, the only thing I can think about is getting lost in her again. I don't want to talk or think or try or plan out our future and how we're going to move along after this. All I want is to ignore it all —wrapped up in her featherlight touch, her quiet giggles, her soft moans and whimpers, and her hot, welcoming body greeting mine like an old friend. She fits me perfectly, like her body was made with me in mind. We're like two pieces from entirely different puzzles that somehow match up perfectly. I don't understand it, but I also don't want to overthink it.

I finish off my drink and exit my office, seeking her out. The living room is empty but her bedroom door is closed. I'm sure that's where she is. I knock twice but open it without waiting for her to tell me to come in or go away. When I step in, she's just stepping out of the bathroom, her body soaked and covered in a towel.

She stands there, motionless, watching as I quickly cross the floor and pull her to me. Our lips meet and she wraps her arms around my neck, not even considering rejecting me. Her hands push my suit jacket over my shoulders and it falls to the floor. She busies herself loosening my tie and unbuttoning my shirt. Her hands finally find my belt and she breaks the kiss, watching her fingers as they unlatch it. I shrug out of my shirt and push my pants down my hips, allowing them to fall into a heap around my ankles. I reach for her towel and one quick tug has it tumbling down her body.

I pull her against me again, kissing her as I step over to the bed. Good thing we're already so close, or I would've had to stop to take off my shoes and pants in order to reach her. I break the kiss and spin her around. Placing my hand on the center of her back, I push her to bend over in front of me. She does as I want and I position myself at her entrance. Without warning, I thrust into her. I slide in with ease, like I'm finally home. I freeze, just cherishing this moment and all the emotions running through my body.

For the first time since I left my grandmother's, I feel like all is right in the world. I can finally breathe. I can finally be me—not the man my grandmother and father raised, but the man she's helping me become. I no longer feel like I'm on top of the world because I have money and nice things. Now, I'm on top of the world because I have her. She makes me a better man in every sense of the word. And while I know I still have a lot to overcome, I want to do it. For her.

All of these things are running through my brain at the same time, and I have no idea what any of it means. But I'm too lost in her to think about it any further. I pull my hips back and thrust them forward again. My hands are on her hips and I let them fall down to her round ass that's bent over in front of me. Her skin is perfect—soft and creamy—slightly lighter than the rest of her body that's been kissed by the sun. There's not a mark on it. Well, not yet anyway.

I bring my hand back and slap the skin. She lets out a loud and startled yelp and turns her head around to find my gaze. I stare back at her as I lift my hand and slap her ass again—only this time, a moan slips from her parted lips that eggs me on to do more. But when I pull my hand away, I see the red print I left behind, and that's what I wanted. I wanted to brand her body as mine, even if the mark will fade away. I grind my hips against her ass as I reach around, my fingers finding her clit. I work steady circles around it, then change it up to go front to back. Her back arches and she throws her head back. While I tease her from the inside out, my other hand finds her breast and I pinch her nipple, wanting to flood her senses with desire and need. I refuse to remove myself from her until she's screaming my name. My release rises quickly, but I hold it back, not ready for this to be over. I like this little world we've created. I don't want to go back to where we started. I want to spend every second of the rest of my life right here in this perfect moment.

Her breathing becomes faster, and her cries get louder. I feel her tighten around me and I lose all control, thrusting into her so violently that we both shatter on impact—nothing but pieces of us both raining down and peppering the ground like broken glass.

When my hips stop, she falls forward, taking me with her as I fall to her side, wrapping her up in my arms. As I work to control my breathing, I kick off my shoes and shimmy out of my pants. Now that we're both completely naked, I crawl up the bed the right way—bringing her with me.

Neither of us has completely found our way back to our bodies yet. We're both still limp—breathing heavily, hearts racing. But neither of us talks or tries to pull away either. Maybe she's feeling the same way I am. I like what we're doing but don't know how to address it and don't want to, fearing I'll screw it all up somehow. We rarely see eye-to-eye on anything. Will this be any different?

After a long, drawn-out silence, she finally speaks. "Your dad is an asshole."

I chuckle. "Yes, he is."

She rolls in my arms so she's looking at me, instead of away from me. "Why does he think you won't follow through?"

I shrug. "He's an asshole, and I guess that's kind of my track record when it comes to him. I was supposed to graduate college and come work for him. Well, I graduated, but I didn't come work for him. I decided against it at the last second. I'm guessing that's what he's referring to."

"So, big deal. You want a life of your own. Why's that so bad?"

"To him, it is. He says he built this business so he could leave it to me. He wanted me to have a son of my own and pass it down the line. But if I don't work there, he can't pass it down to me. Which means his whole plan to be remembered forever is already failing."

"So all of this anger and resentment is because you're living your own life and not the one he set up for you? I mean, you're a Harvard-educated lawyer—not exactly a disappointment."

"That's exactly it," I agree.

She looks up, her eyes meeting mine as her hand comes up to cup my jaw. "You're a better man than he is. Don't forget that."

She closes the space between our lips and kisses me softly, sucking the air straight from my lungs. I've barely let her in—only given her small glimpses into my life—and she already knows this? How? She doesn't know everything I've been through. She doesn't know why I act the way I do, but somehow she's found a way to see past all the bad and find the only good spot that's left inside me. With each touch, each kiss, and each word whispered between us, that spot grows. I can only hope that one day it eats up the bad, leaving me to be the man she needs—the man she's suddenly opened herself up to.

———

THE WEEKEND PASSES QUICKLY and Monday rolls around. Back to the office we go. But today feels different than previous days. We've shared a piece of ourselves this past weekend, and it's changed everything in our future, even though neither of us has talked about what that change means.

We laugh and joke and talk on the way to the office. When we get there, we head inside to find the place locked up and quiet. Daniel hasn't made it in yet, so I hang out by her desk while she gets prepared for the day. I watch as she turns on her computer and gets the phones going. She pulls up the appointment book and stands to gather the needed files for the day. I get overwhelmed by the amount of time I've gone without touching her, so I push her up against the filing cabinets and press my chest to hers as I kiss her breathless.

"Matthew, we shouldn't be doing this here," she says against my lips, but makes no attempt to push me away.

"You're right. Let's go to my office," I reply, my hands already trying to work their way up her skirt.

Someone clears their throat from behind me and I turn my head to find Daniel standing in front of her desk with a wide grin. "Can I talk to you for a minute?" he asks.

I turn back to her. "Hold that thought," I whisper, pulling away and motioning for Daniel to lead the way.

I follow him into my office and close the door behind us. "What's up?" I ask, walking around my desk to take a seat while he sits in the chair on the opposite side.

"What the hell was that?" he asks, eyes wide with surprise and mouth turned up into a smile.

"Oh, that was . . . nothing." I don't know how else to explain it. I mean, what do I say? I can't tell him we're just having a fling. That could end badly, then the office would be shorthanded. I can't tell him we're dating, because we haven't even agreed to that yet. I don't know what the fuck we're doing. All I know is that I don't want it to stop.

"Nothing?" he questions. "That didn't look like nothing. That looked like something. Are you guys dating now?"

"What? No." Deny, deny, deny.

"Are you just . . . fucking around? Hooking up?"

I let out a long breath and lean in to talk at a quieter volume. "I don't know what the fuck we're doing, man. We've been hanging out more. She's—well, she's helping me out with a problem. And hanging out so much has been really good for us. We're getting along better than we ever have, and that's only made the attraction I've felt toward her grow."

"Whoa, what attraction? You told me you could have 12 just like her."

I laugh at the words he's throwing back in my face. "That was a lie and we both know it."

He laughs but stops to wrap his mind around this whole thing. "Okay, so I'm guessing you've hooked up?"

I nod. "This last weekend. We got into another argument and I don't know what happened. We ended up sleeping together."

"And then?" he raises a brow.

"And then we woke up and did it again."

He smirks and shakes his head. "And then?"

"Then we got up and went to brunch at my grandmother's house. We didn't talk about it."

"Come on, Matt. Give me something to work with here. What happened after that?"

"After that?" I think back to yesterday. "I got into a fight with my dad so we left brunch. We got back to the house and I went to cool off alone in my office, but all I could think about was her. So I went into her bedroom and we slept together again. After that, the rest of the day, we just spent in bed—talking, laughing, and doing it again and again and again—"

"All right, I get the picture," he interrupts. "So she's staying with you?" he asks, suddenly confused.

Oh, I forgot he wasn't aware of our arrangement. "Oh, um, yeah. Just for the time being. You know, while she helps me with that thing."

"What thing?"

Her voice comes over the speaker. "Mr. Newton is here for your meeting. Should I send him in?"

Thank God I don't have to answer that question.

"Sorry, pal. I've gotta work." I stand up and show him to the door.

"We're talking about this later," he says.

I smile and nod, but have no intention of doing so. "Mr. Newton, right back here, sir." I show the man to my office, taking a longing look at Poppy and those fucking red heels before closing the door between us.

SEVENTEEN

POPPY

I'm sitting at my desk, staring blankly at the computer screen and tapping my pen off the keyboard. I know I should be working, but honestly, I'm too confused to work. It's driving me crazy that I don't know what this thing between Matthew and me is. I mean, he seems just as into it as I do. Especially after he sought me out in my bedroom yesterday. And then again last night after we went our separate ways to sleep. I was almost sound asleep when I heard the soft clicking of my door opening and shutting. Moments later, his hot body was pressed against my back, his strong arms wrapping around me. He didn't try for sex and neither did I. Instead, we just held each other all night long. I've never slept so well in all my life.

But that has me questioning his intentions and reading into things. Does he want more? Does he want a relationship? What's the meaning behind all of this? And what exactly do *I* want? I want Matthew, but I want *my* version of him. He isn't just one-sided, and that's the problem. With the good comes the bad. And I'm not sure if he wants the real me or the fake image of me he has in his head: the one who wears expensive jewelry and goes to the gym and the spa. That's not the real me. Or has he finally been able to see past that?

The worst part about all of this is that I'm afraid to even ask—as if asking will break the magical spell we're under and everything will go back to the way it was before.

And even though I'm confused about everything between us, I don't stop to think when he sticks his head out of his office door and motions for me to join him. I smile, my stomach tightening and filling with butterflies as I stand and walk inside the room. The moment we're alone, he tugs me against him and kisses me senseless. He carries me across the floor and bends me over the front of his desk.

"Those shoes drive me mad," he says, freeing himself from his pants. He begins pushing my skirt up my legs, allowing his hand to run up the length of my leg—all the way to my ass. "And this fucking red lace thong to match . . ." he yanks it down. "Are you trying to kill me?" he asks, taking himself in hand and shoving into me.

"Oh," I breathe out the moment his hips are pressing into my ass.

"You have no idea how many times I've imagined doing this." He thrusts back in again—harder, deeper. "Those shoes have run miles in my head." He grinds his hips into me, making me bite down on my lower lip to keep from calling out.

"Fuck, you feel so good. Do you like that?" he asks, squeezing my hips as he pushes into me.

I feel like playing the part of the good little secretary. "Yes, sir," I reply. This only makes him let out a growl as his hips work faster. He clearly liked that, so I keep going. "Oh, Mr. Lewis . . ."

Another growl fills my ears as his hips become erratic.

"Yes, don't stop," I beg, more for his sake than mine. What's he's doing feels good, but I'm nowhere near ready to finish and I can tell that this was meant to be a quickie. He'll have to owe me one after this go-round.

He lets out a sound that's a mix between a moan and a growl as he explodes into me. He pounds out every last wave of his release, hips jerking and sputtering to a stop. Finally, he freezes behind me.

He removes himself from me and tucks himself back into his

pants as I stand up, pushing my skirt back into place. I look up and meet his eyes. He's smirking and he draws closer.

"I really liked that dirty secretary stuff." He kisses me.

I giggle against his lips. "I thought you would."

I pull away and walk around the desk to leave his office, but he catches me at the door for one more kiss. "Maybe we can do that at home later?"

"We better. You owe me one."

He pulls back out of surprise. "I owe you one?" he asks. "You usually get off three or four times while I only get off once. If anyone has achieved higher numbers, it's you," he says around a smile as he opens the door.

I go to step out, but find Daniel standing there, arms crossed and smiling wide. Matthew and I both stand frozen in place.

"My office," he tells Matthew. He looks back at me. "Poppy, I ordered us all some lunch from the Italian place down the street. Would you mind picking it up?"

"No problem," I agree, heading to my desk to get my things.

It's not until I walk outside that I realize I don't have my panties. Shit. I can't go back in there. Not now. Not after we've been caught. Surely he knows exactly what all that noise was, even though I was trying to be quiet. My face grows hot as the embarrassment takes over. I pick up the speed of my walking, almost like I can walk it off or outrun it, but that isn't the case. Embarrassment is faster than my legs and it can't be outrun.

———

"SO, what did Daniel have to say today?" I ask when we get in the car to drive home.

He looks at me then moves his eyes away to start the car. "I don't want to talk about it."

"Is he mad? Did he know what we were doing? Oh! That

reminds me . . . I left my panties in there. I've been commando all day."

He looks back at me now, grin in place. "I know," he says, reaching into his pocket and pulling out my red lace thong.

I gasp and grab for it, but he pulls it out of reach. "Oh no. I've been holding on to this as a reminder that I owe you one."

I giggle. "You've had my panties in your pocket all afternoon?"

"Mm-hmm. And every time I put my hand in my pocket, I managed to excite myself. Wasn't bad until I forgot and did it during a meeting. I couldn't stand up to show the guy to the door."

I laugh harder at this.

"Oh, you laugh now, but when we get home, I'm fucking you into exhaustion. You'll have to beg me to stop making you come."

My body flashes with heat and my muscles tighten with anticipation. But when we get home, I don't regret a minute of it. It seems we've found our new game: tease each other all day so we combust when we get home. And I don't plan on losing.

The next day, while Matthew is in the middle of a meeting, he calls my desk phone to ask me to give him some paperwork. Instead of answering him in words, I moan softly into the phone. I hear a loud thud come from his office, which I can also hear through the phone. I don't know what it was, but I have a feeling it was a direct response to that moan. I top it off with an "I need you now," which I say in a breathy moan.

I hear him clear his throat then whisper, "If you think I can get up and retrieve that paperwork now, you're very mistaken."

I giggle. "I'm coming," I say just as breathlessly, then hang up the phone and gather the paperwork he needs. I walk into his office and set it down on his desk. "Here you go, Mr. Lewis. Everything you asked for."

His jaw tightens and his eyes narrow, their depths deeper than any ocean. "Thank you," he replies, watching me as I walk out, swaying my ass a little more than necessary.

When his client leaves, he walks him out, waves goodbye, and looks at me once we're alone. "I'm going to get you back for that."

I just smile and giggle.

"I have to go out for a moment. What time is my next appointment?"

I look down at the screen. "Forty-five minutes. Where are you going?"

He grins. "It's a surprise. I'll be right back." He walks out, leaving me wondering what he has up his sleeve.

Thirty minutes later, he's back with a small black bag tucked under his arm. He motions for me to join him in his office and I do so gladly, needing to know what's in the bag. I step inside as he closes the door, takes my wrist, and directs me over to his desk. He drops down to his knees before me.

Oh!

He reaches up my skirt and pulls my panties down my legs, so I step out of them for him. But instead of moving my skirt out of the way to get to the goods, he opens the bag and pulls out new panties. He motions for me to step into them and I do so, confused.

"What's the point of this?" I ask, suddenly feeling let down. "I thought we were going to have some fun."

"We are," he replies, looking up at me from his place on the floor.

"How is this fun?"

"Well," he says, standing up now and reaching into his pocket. "You seem to think it's fun to tease me when I can't do anything about it, so I thought I'd have some fun of my own." That's when the hand in his pocket moves and a strong vibration goes off between my legs. I jump and he laughs.

He pulls the remote out of his pocket and shows it to me. "Whenever I feel like I may need some attention from you, I'm going to press this little button." His finger moves to the button, pressing it and making my panties vibrate. My eyes nearly roll into the back of my head.

"You can't expect me to wear these all day long! What if I just go into the bathroom and take them off?"

"If you're not wearing these panties when we get home, I won't touch you for the rest of the evening."

My mouth drops open. "What? You can't be serious."

"Oh, I'm very serious. Now, you may go back to your desk. Leave the door open. I want to hear you when I press this button."

With a huff, I turn on my heel and leave his office, taking a seat at my desk.

EIGHTEEN

MATTHEW

It would be too much fun to press this button the moment she sits down. But she'll be expecting that. No, I plan on waiting until she's managed to forget what she's wearing—maybe a moment when she needs to be on the phone or addressing a client. That sounds like a lot more fun to me.

I set down the remote and get back to work, combing through piles and piles of paperwork. I get completely lost in it and forget all about the power I have sitting on the side of my desk—that is, until I hear the main office door open. My next client has arrived.

"Hello, Mr. Baron. I'll let Mr. Lewis know that you've—" I hit the button. *"Arrived!"* she yells, making the old man jump.

I can't hold back my laugh as she comes walking up to my door, legs squeezed together like she's going to pee her pants at any second.

"Stop that!" she whisper-yells.

I take my finger off the button and put it down. "Your client is here," she breathes out, her eyes as dark as midnight.

"Show him in, please."

Mr. Baron enters and we shake hands as he takes a seat in front of me.

"What can I do for you, Mr. Baron?" I ask, but my eyes catch a glimpse of the remote on my desk and I pick it up, turning it over and over in my hands as I listen.

"I'd like to make some changes to my will. My wife just passed away and I need to move everything to my children's names."

"I'm very sorry to hear that, but I think we can get everything taken care of quickly and easily."

He nods as I lean forward and start tapping on the keyboard, leaving the remote in my lap. I pull up the documents we need and print them off using the printer on the other end of my desk. I start explaining the paperwork—showing him how we're taking one name off and replacing it with the names of his children. I watch as he signs the paper that states he's authorizing this change, then he has to look everything over to ensure it's correct, and sign again. As I'm waiting for him to approve of everything, the phone on my desk rings. How odd. She never calls when I'm with a client unless it's urgent. I pick up. "Yes?"

She's breathless. "Please, please stop pushing the button. I've already come three times."

"What? I'm not pushing . . ." Then I look down at my lap and see that the remote is no longer there. It fell between my legs, and after so much shifting back and forth in my chair, it somehow wedged itself beneath me. I'm sitting on the remote. I lift up and she lets out a sigh. "Thank you," she breathes out.

I can't hold back my laughter. "I'm sorry. It wasn't my intention."

"Mm-hmm." She doesn't buy it. Instead, she just hangs up the phone.

I wrap things up with Mr. Baron and show him to the door. Then I turn to face Poppy.

"I'm so sorry. I was sitting on the remote."

"Yeah, well, that was perfect timing, because I was actually booking you an appointment when it went off."

"Over the phone?" I smirk, imagining what that person thought.

"No, not over the phone. He was a walk-in!"

This makes me laugh harder. She stands back, letting me get it all out. Finally, when I can no longer breathe, I'm able to stand up and dry the tears from my eyes.

She smirks. "I really don't know why you're laughing. I came in front of some guy! He knows my 'O' face thanks to you!"

I want to find that funny but I can't. Instead, I'm instantly annoyed that some man saw her in a way only I'm supposed to see her.

"He really liked the performance. He gave me his number and told me to call him. He said that if I get that excited about booking an appointment, then I'd probably get *really* happy about a date!" She picks up a piece of paper and shows it to me. It has a phone number and the name above it reads *John Parker*.

"Fuck this guy," I say, crumpling the paper and tossing it into the trash can.

She holds out her hand. "Can I have the remote now?"

I slide my hand into my pocket where the remote is and hold it tight. "No. It's mine."

"You still want to play this game after that mistake?"

I think it over. No, but I like the idea of her being teased and waiting for me all day. "I promise I'll be more careful. I swear."

She takes a deep breath, but I can see she's giving me the benefit of the doubt. "Fine, but another slip-up like that one and it'll be me who doesn't touch you tonight."

I reluctantly agree and go back into my office. As I sit behind my desk, holding the remote in my hand, I can't help but wonder how wet she is right now. Three times? She got off three times while I was in that one meeting? I'm going to have to be more careful, or she's going to be exhausted before we even get home. But fuck, I bet her pussy is glowing pink and glistening right now. I can't help but lick my lips. My will to hold out on her until we get home is crumbling. Now more than before, I want to fuck her so hard against my desk that we move it across the room. My dick hardens in my pants just from thinking about it.

I hit the button and hear a thump. She probably jumped and hit her knee on the bottom of the desk. I figure I'll just hit the button once every 10 minutes or so. This will keep her on her toes so she's more than ready for me by the time we get to come together.

She seems stiff as we walk across the street to go into the parking garage. Neither of us speaks as we climb into the car, and when she sits down, she crosses her legs like she needs all the added pressure she can get. I smirk to myself but don't mention it as I drive us back home for the day.

The moment we walk in the door, she's spinning around and jumping into my arms. Her legs wrap around my hips and I hear her skirt tear, but that doesn't stop either of us. My hands land on her ass as I carry her into my room. I kick the door shut behind us and start stripping out of my jacket as we kiss. She's holding on so tight, I don't even have to hold her. Once the jacket hits the floor, my hands find her thighs, moving upward until I find the rip up the seam. I place a hand on each side, pulling in opposite directions. The fabric rips up the middle and I pull it out from between us.

I toss it to the side and lay her down on the bed. Our kiss breaks momentarily as I free myself from my pants. Her panties are still in my way, and in my haste to be inside her, I yank at them. The thin lace rips, but at least she's bare now, allowing me to thrust inside her. As I expected, the junction between her legs is pink and glistening with her arousal. We both let out a moan at the sensation of finally being together again. We've been welded together more often than not lately. In fact, it's to the point where it just doesn't feel right if we're not together.

Her arm reaches around my neck and pulls my mouth back to hers while I move in and out of her. One hand is cupping the back of her head while the other is grasping her hip, pulling her into my thrusts. I'm breathless from our kiss, and that's making me dizzy, but it's a sensation I crave. I don't dare break our kiss. I can already feel her muscles tightening around me, driving me mad with need. I don't need to get off myself—well, I do, but that's not what's driving me. I need to make her come undone around me. I need to watch the passion and pleasure reach her face and change her emotions. I need to feel her milking my dick for every last drop. I need to feel her hot breath against my skin and her loud moans filling my ears. All of my needs suddenly revolve around her.

She shatters around me and I burn every aspect into my memory —sear it there to keep it locked away forever. I don't know where the future will take us, but I know whether I get to keep her or not, I'll always have this.

Thinking about taking this moment and placing it in a glass jar that I can forever keep on a shelf inside my head pushes me over the edge, and my release rises to the surface. My hips start to move at their own pace and my thrusting becomes erratic as I lose all control of my body. My head climbs high into the clouds as my heart races to catch up. My orgasm comes rushing out of me like a freight train: fast, uncontrollable, and loud as I call out her name. Her name falls from my lips like a prayer. A name I once spit out in disgust is a name I now crave saying.

I collapse on top of her and she holds me close as we both work to regain control of our bodies. I can feel her heart racing right alongside mine. Her lungs are working harder to get the air she needs.

"Fuck, Poppy," I breathe out as I remove myself from her. "Remind me to buy more of those panties."

She giggles. "Why do we need more than one pair?"

"You can't wear the same panties every day, now can you?"

She laughs and playfully smacks my chest. "No way am I giving you control of my panties every day. You just about killed me today."

"Come on, I like knowing you're horny and craving me all day."

Her eyes meet mine. "You don't need a remote for that."

I reach out and pull her against my chest, breathing in her scent—

perfume mixed with sweat and sex. I feel like her scent is burned into my nostrils, but it's a burn I crave, and one I miss when I've gone too long without inhaling her. I'm fairly certain I'm beyond addicted to her—now a junkie praying for his next fix and counting down the minutes until I can have her time and time again.

NINETEEN

POPPY

Minutes spent with him feel like seconds. Time passes too quickly—speeding up when we're together and slowing down when we have to be apart during work mode, while our evenings are bittersweet, knowing our time is limited. Our week passes by in a mix of rushed minutes and dragging seconds. Friday rolls around again and we're making our way back to his grandmother's house for dinner.

"Will your father be attending?" I ask as we hold hands on our drive.

He doesn't look away from the road as he answers. "I don't know, but I doubt it. He always has an excuse to get out of dinner."

"But brunch is a different story?"

"Gran won't let him get out of both, and he'd rather spend his Friday nights working late at the office."

"How's her health doing? Any updates?" I ask because this thing we're doing is for her benefit, and I want to know when I need to start pulling away so our separation will be as easy as possible for me. I'm sure he'll be fine getting his life and home back to normal, but recently, I've found myself getting too comfortable. I have to keep reminding myself that this isn't real. He isn't falling in love with me. This situation is just convenient for him, and even though that saddens me slightly, I'm okay with it because I knew what I was signing up for. I don't wish for forever with him. I can't. I'm not entitled to it after this short amount of time. I've already gotten more than I expected. But I do hope that when this ends—when we each go back to our normal lives—that he keeps a small piece of me with him. I hope he continues to be the man he only shows to me.

"She went to the doctor yesterday. They're keeping a close eye on her, but they've noted some recent declines. Slow but steady."

"Well, she seems to be getting around just fine."

He lets out a deep chuckle. "That old lady is too mean. She won't go down without a fight. She will kick and scream the whole way. She refuses to let us put her in a home or help her in any way. She's a tough old bat. And, well, as long as she's able to take care of herself, with help from her staff, why try forcing her into something she doesn't want?"

"You're a good grandson."

He gives me a small but shy smile. "I'd do anything for her. She's like a mother to me."

We make it over to her house and he opens my door like a true gentleman. On our walk to the door, his hand is on the small of my back, leading the way. He reaches forward and rings the doorbell, then leans in to whisper in my ear. "You look beautiful, by the way."

My cheeks heat up with his praise.

"I really like this dress." His hand falls from my lower back to my ass, then over its curve and to my thigh, where he pulls the dress up slightly like he's about to have his way with me, but the door opens and he quickly removes his hand and stands upright with a smile in place.

"Good evening, Mr. Matthew," the maid says, welcoming us in. "Ms. Poppy."

I smile as I take off my coat and hand it over along with my purse. "How have you been?"

"Very well, thank you," she replies, taking our things. "Mrs. Lewis is already in the lounge. You may go on in if you'd like."

"Thank you," Matthew says, hand back on me and leading me in the direction of the lounge.

We walk into the lounge and his grandmother is sitting in her chair like normal. She seems pale today, her skin nearly transparent with a greenish sheen to it. She has dark circles under her eyes and her lips are white around the edges.

"How you feeling today, Gran?" Matthew asks, taking his seat.

"Not the best, dear. That doctor has changed my medication again and he says it could take several days for my body to adjust."

"If you don't feel up to dinner . . ." Matthew starts, but she cuts him off.

"Nonsense. I know you might think I don't have very many of these dinners left, but whether or not that's the case, I'm going to enjoy every last one of them." Her eyes cut to me and she winks. "And I hope we're still on for tea this Sunday?"

I nod and smile. "Absolutely, but if you don't feel up to it . . ."

"I will be there with bells on," she insists, then looks at Matthew. "You father won't be attending dinner again this evening."

"I didn't figure he would," Matthew replies.

"I wish he would open his eyes and see that this is the most important place to be—with family. Not sitting at some desk all alone."

Matthew lifts his hand and places it on his knee. "You know how he is, Gran. Always work and never any play."

"Well, you two look like you're getting closer," she notices.

I look over at Matthew and notice that we are sitting closer than we have in the past. He has one hand on my knee and my hand is covering his. He looks over at me as our eyes simultaneously fall to our hands, then back up to each other's eyes. He lets out a nervous chuckle and removes his hand.

"Well, don't let me come between you. Intimacy is important in a marriage."

My face heats. I don't know about a marriage, but there *has* been plenty of intimacy lately.

"That's okay, Gran," he tells her. "I honestly didn't even realize how inappropriate I was behaving."

She smiles a sweet, kind smile. "That's the best kind, isn't it? When you crave the touch of another person so much that you reach for them without even realizing you're doing it?" She points at us. "I have a good feeling about the two of you. I think you'll have a long and fruitful marriage. I can only pray that I last long enough to meet my grandchildren."

My back straightens and I suddenly feel a little jittery.

Matthew lets out a nervous laugh. "We . . . uh . . . well, we haven't really decided if we want kids or not, Gran. It's something we plan to discuss later on down the line."

"Later?" she gasps. "These are important issues, Matthew! What if you want kids and Poppy doesn't? Or what if she wants kids and you don't? These things should've been discussed before you even asked for her hand. You have to make sure you're compatible in every aspect."

"Oh, we're very compatible," I blurt out, then immediately regret it. Matthew's eyes flash to mine and I can see the question in them: *Why the hell did you say that?*

"That's nice, dear. But I meant compatible outside of the bedroom."

"Gran . . ." Matthew breathes out in embarrassment.

"What? You act like I don't know what a man and wife do. I was married for 57 years, you know."

"Dinner is served," the maid comes in and says.

"Thank God," Matthew says under his breath as we all stand. He goes over to his grandmother and helps her from her seat. She seems to need more help than she has in the past.

"Thank you. This medicine just makes me so dizzy," she says, shuffling across the hardwood floor.

We all make it to the dining room and take our seats. Dinner is served, and as usual, it's delicious and decadent. The food is always served with wine, and without fail, there's some kind of fancy dessert I've never tried before but love just the same. Tonight's conversation flows easily, his grandmother now involving me more and more with each passing week. It seems like she's suddenly welcomed me into the family with open arms—like I've always been here. The awkwardness from before has faded away, now replaced with warmth, acceptance, and love.

The dinner ends at 9 p.m., and we leave on the dot. She doesn't even bother showing us to the door. She's ready for bed and a staff member helps her upstairs while another shows us out. The two of us get back in the car, where we're surrounded by darkness.

"Your grandmother is very sweet," I say, staring up at the night sky that's midnight blue with millions of tiny, brightly-lit stars. There's only a sliver of a moon tonight, making the stars burn that much brighter in its absence.

He chuckles under his breath. "You haven't seen the real granny yet. Just wait until she needs another hospital stay. She'll turn from being sweet as candy to rotten as a candy apple a week after Halloween."

I smile and shrug. "Can't we all do that, though? I know you can, and you've seen me at my worst."

"I have?" he asks.

"Like you could forget . . ."

He draws his brows together, wracking his brain for any moment when I may have been anything less than pleasant.

"The car," I point out.

He laughs. "Oh, right. How could I forget that? I get it back tomorrow afternoon. Stay away from my baby."

I giggle. "Better not piss me off again."

"We both know the odds of that."

"Then she's still not safe," I joke.

"So it looks like we're going to be faking a marriage too . . . not just an engagement."

I know he's joking, but I can't help but think about it. Damaging his car is what got me here: faking this engagement and ending up in his bed. If I do it again, maybe that would be a reason to keep me around longer. Maybe forever? I chuckle at the silly thought. But how long can I pretend I don't enjoy being with him? I think I've already dropped the ball on that one. I think he knows how much I like being with him like this, in our fake engagement—not only sharing our lives but sharing our beds too.

But it's more than just sex. Over these last couple weeks, I've seen him become softer, less angry. I've watched him give up that control he always seemed to need. He's given me trust and friendship as he's become someone I feel I can count on and lean on. I never would've guessed when I smashed the shit out of his priceless sports car with his fancy golf club that this is where we'd end up. But now that we're here, I'm afraid to leave. I want things to stay this way. Just thinking about going our separate ways has a hole opening in my stomach. And that makes me wonder if he feels the same way. He seems to enjoy my company as much as I've been enjoying his.

How will this end for us?

Forever happy and in love . . . or nothing but heartbreak?

TWENTY

MATTHEW

Saturday rolls around and I sneak out of bed, leaving Poppy to sleep. I watch the clock, counting down the minutes until the delivery men arrive with her surprise. I'm pacing back and forth in front of the door, watching the seconds tick by on the clock that hangs above the fireplace. The delivery information sheet stated that they would be here at 8 a.m., and it's now 7:54. Poppy doesn't ever sleep past 8 on weekdays and 9 on weekends, but I want everything set up before she wakes. That way, when she walks out of the bedroom, the first thing she'll see is the brand-new grand piano I've purchased for her.

Sure, I know she won't have room for it in her apartment when she returns, but it'll always be here and it'll always be hers. But maybe by the end of this, she won't want to return. She doesn't act like she's being forced to stay here anymore. She seems to feel more welcome—more at home. I would love for my house to become her home too, but that just leads me to think of things I'd rather not. I haven't tried to figure out the end of this just yet. All I know is that what I first thought I wanted is no longer enough. I don't just want her in my bed for one night anymore. I want her in my bed every night. Every fucking night for the rest of my life. Anything less will never be enough.

My cell rings with a call from the doorman downstairs alerting me to a delivery. I tell him to send them up, excited that the piano is finally here and she hasn't come out of the bedroom yet. I might just pull this off. The elevator doors open and two men are standing at my door dressed in coveralls and holding clipboards.

"You Mr. Lewis?"

"I am."

"We have a delivery for you. Grand piano?"

"You're at the right place," I tell them, waving them in as I unlatch the second half of the double door.

"Where would you like us to put it?" one man asks.

I point over to the area in front of the windows. "Anywhere over there will suffice."

He nods. "Very well."

The two men walk out, and they're back a little while later with the piano on a big rolling cart. One is pushing and the other is pulling; both of them look tired and out of breath.

"She's so big, you're lucky your elevator is the size of a service elevator," one grunts out, steering the big cart over to the area I indicated.

The cart they're using is pretty amazing. They put it in place, then hit a couple of buttons. The top part of the cart, where the four legs of the piano are sitting, lifts up, moves to the side, then lowers to the floor. Once the piano is in place, they each take turns lifting up the legs to get the section of cart out from under them. The piano is in place within minutes. By 8:07, the two men are walking out. I tipped them extra for being relatively quiet.

With everything now ready, I go back into the bedroom, crawl up on the bed, and pull her to my chest. She snuggles against me, a sleepy smile on her face.

"Good morning, beautiful," I whisper, nuzzling my face into her hair.

"Good morning," she replies with a grin as she stretches.

"I have a surprise for you," I whisper.

"You do?"

"Mm-hmm. Want to come see it?"

She smiles widely now and nods.

I wait on the bed while she gets up and uses the bathroom, then I lead her into the living room. She steps inside and her eyes start on the right side, sweeping over the entryway and the dining room, followed by the fireplace, couch, tables, and TV. Then her view goes to the center of the room, where she finds nothing but the swinging door to the kitchen. Finally, she looks toward the windows and gasps as she discovers the shiny black grand piano. Her eyes are wide and sparkling with excitement, and her lips are turned up into the most beautiful smile I've ever seen her wear.

"This is for me?" she asks, covering her face, which is growing red.

"Yup," I say, taking her hands from her face and pulling her over to it. "What do you think?"

"It's . . . beautiful," she breathes out, looking over every inch. "I only wish I knew how to play. Something this beautiful has to be played—not just looked at."

"Take a seat," I say, pulling her over to the bench, and she does as I ask. "I've hired someone to give you lessons, if you're interested."

Her eyes turn to mine. "Really?"

I laugh and nod. "Yes, I thought it was about time you finally got to do something you've always wanted to."

She offers up a soft smile. "Thank you," she says quietly, leaning in and brushing her lips against mine. The kiss is soft and teasing, and I can't help but wonder if this is how things could always be with us. I pull away before the thoughts can go too far. "Play me something."

She rolls her eyes but places her fingers on the keys. Slowly—and terribly, I might add—she starts playing "Twinkle, Twinkle, Little Star." She plays the whole song then lets her hands fall into her lap.

"I'm not very good," she says, looking down at her hands like a child who's in trouble. "Okay, I'm awful."

I place my hand under her chin and tilt her head back until our eyes meet. "It was beautiful, just like you. Will you play it again?" I give her a smile and she quickly returns it before starting up the song for a second time.

The two of us spend the day sitting at the piano and playing around. Neither of us knows how to play properly, but that doesn't stop us from having fun. We play, talk, and laugh as the hours just fly by. The next thing I know, I'm getting a call. I pull my phone from my pocket and answer it.

"Hello?"

"Mr. Lewis?"

"Yes."

"This is Johnny from the Audi dealership. I'm just calling to let you know your car is all finished. You can come and get her."

"Wonderful news. Thank you."

"Who was that?" she asks when I hang up the phone.

"The dealership. I can go pick up the car. Want to ride along? Finally sit in the thing you destroyed?"

She giggles. "Sure, but I'll need to get dressed."

"That makes two of us."

We each go to our rooms to get dressed for the day. When she walks out, I can't do anything but watch her walk closer to me. Her long legs are accentuated by black skinny jeans that look painted on. The knees are ripped out and there are random slashes across them, giving me small peeks at her skin. She's wearing a pair of ankle boots, a tight crimson shirt, and a black leather jacket. She looks hot as hell.

"Why are you staring at me?" she asks, blushing as she looks down at herself.

"I didn't realize I was." I shake my head clear of all the dirty thoughts she suddenly pushed into it. "Ready?"

She laughs. "You're so weird, but yes. Let's go pick up my competition."

I snort as I take her hand in mine. "There's no competition."

"She'll win every time, huh?" she asks with a hint of amusement in her voice.

"Not even close," I reply, pulling her toward the door.

It's easy to see that Poppy doesn't see what I do when I look at her. I guess that's my past self's fault. I didn't treat her very well before, and the funny thing is, I didn't even care. I couldn't be bothered to care. In my eyes, she was nothing but a frustration—a constant screw-up. But these last couple of weeks have changed me in more ways than I thought possible. I was born and raised to think that if you didn't have money, you didn't matter. I didn't realize that was something I could even overcome or change my way of thinking about. But that's the kind of person Poppy is. She's good to the core. She doesn't look down on anyone. In her eyes, everyone is on exactly the same playing field, with no one person ranking higher than another. She does good and brings out the good in others around her.

We pick up the car and I can't help but want to spend a little time behind the wheel. We take a long drive through the city and all around it, cruising slowly to enjoy some sites while speeding through others. The speed feels good, giving me back my control. Everything about this car feels good—even the way the leather seats cup your ass. Poppy just sits beside me and lets me enjoy having my baby back. She doesn't even complain about the speed, although I can see her white-knuckling the door handle. She knows that I'm enjoying myself, and I think she's even enjoying herself a little too.

We drive until it gets dark and both of us start to feel hungry. Neither of us feels up to a sit-down place, and frankly, I don't feel like parking my newly restored car on the street. So we end up swinging by a Chinese restaurant and order just about everything on the menu to take back home. I hate to admit it, but eating dinner with her on the couch is something I'm really starting to like. This couldn't be any further from how I was raised. All meals were to be consumed in the dining room. No exceptions. But now she's showing me a whole new way to live, and it's something I find myself craving more and more.

"Did you really have to order the whole menu? That's wasteful," she reminds me as she holds all the bags in her lap.

"Truth be told, the restaurant would've wasted it all at the end of the night anyway. This way, at least I'm paying an independently-owned restaurant and thus supporting a small business." I offer up a smile and she can't argue with that. She just laughs and rolls her eyes.

We get home and spread everything out on the coffee table and dig in, eating straight from the cartons rather than using plates. "So, are you looking forward to high tea with my grandmother tomorrow?"

She snorts. "I'm not really a high tea person, but I guess it would be cool to get to know her. And honestly, I have no idea what high tea even is. Is the queen gonna be there?"

"Want a tip?"

Her eyes widen. "Yes, please!"

"Don't bring up the fact that she's dying. Don't bring up her health at all, actually. She really hates it when she feels like she's being pitied."

Her mouth drops open. "Of course I wouldn't bring that up! What kind of person do you think I am?"

I laugh. "I'm not saying you would. I just wanted to warn you in case something comes up." I shrug and dive back into my food.

My phone rings and I slide it out of my pocket to see my father calling. "Hello?" I answer.

"Matthew, a courier should be there any minute to deliver some important information. I just wanted to make sure you were there to accept the package."

"What package? What are you sending me?" I ask, still annoyed from the last time we talked.

"You'll see. Just look it over and call me back. Alone, if you would."

"All right, Dad. Fine," I agree, hanging up the phone.

"Everything okay?" Poppy asks, tearing her eyes away from the TV.

"Yes, just more games from my father." Moments later, the doorbell is ringing and I excuse myself to go answer it. I'm given a thick envelope, at which point I go directly to my office with it. I sit behind my desk and open the envelope. I pull out a big file that probably weighs five pounds.

Rolling my eyes, I open it to see a picture of Poppy on top. I flip through the pages, seeing report cards, past debts, current debts, her bank account information, and a ton of shit about her parents as well: banking information, insurance documents, and debts upon debts upon debts.

I grab my phone and call my dad immediately.

"Hello?" he answers.

"What the fuck is this shit?" I ask, pissed off and annoyed that he's going to such lengths to ensure I don't marry Poppy.

"You know exactly what it is. Look at that file and tell me that's a woman who's good enough to marry."

I shake my head and close the file. "This is none of your business."

"None of my business? You're my only son. Damn straight, it's my business."

"Why? How? I'm not working for you. I'm not living off of you. Hell, I don't even see you. How is my relationship your business?"

"You think I'm going to leave everything I've got to a son who's marrying a gold digger? That's all she is, son. With her debt and her parents' debt, you'll lose everything. And all my hard work isn't getting stolen once I'm on my deathbed."

"Then leave that shit to someone else. I don't want it. I told you that years ago. And stay the hell away from my fiancée." I hang up the phone and sit back in my chair, quietly seething.

TWENTY-ONE

POPPY

I don't know what's going on, but Matthew has been in his office for nearly an hour. He didn't even finish eating dinner. I leave everything on the table because I don't want to put it away if he isn't done, and I take a shower, thinking he'll be done with whatever he's doing by the time I get out. I wash, shave, and dress in my normal long T-shirt and panties. When I step out of my room, his office door is still closed.

Wanting to check to make sure he's okay, I knock on the door.

"Come in," he says dejectedly from the other side.

I open the door, stepping in halfway. "I didn't want to clean up the food if you're not done." I motion toward the living room.

He shakes his head slightly. "I completely forgot. I've been dealing with my father's bullshit."

"Everything okay?" I ask, noticing that the fine lines between and around his eyes are more visible than usual.

He nods and lets out a long, deep breath. "Just . . . my father. I'm always surprised by the lengths he goes to, although I'm not sure why anymore. There's no hoop too big for him to jump through."

I nod, not wanting to be pushy or butt into his family business. "Well, I'm pretty tired, so I think I'm just going to go to bed."

"Come here," he demands quietly.

As I walk toward his desk, he scoots his chair back and I sit on his lap. He looks deeply into my eyes for a long moment. I begin to wonder what he's thinking, but then his hand comes up to cup my cheek. Slowly, he leans in, his lips finding mine.

This kiss isn't like most of our kisses. Usually, when we come together, it's out of desperation. It's always fast and hard and rushed. But this kiss is soft and slow—teasing not only my body but my heart and mind too. I get lost in this kiss, in him. I take it deeper, enjoying the feeling of his soft lips on mine—that slight hint of brandy on his breath, and the way his hands feel against my skin. I lift myself up, placing a leg on either side of him so I can face him directly.

Now that we're face-to-face, with me on his lap, he leans forward, arms wrapping around my waist. His hands fall down to my ass as he gathers my shirt in his hands, finding the exposed skin of my ass beneath it. Everything about this man enthralls me. He captures my attention and never releases it. I'm his prisoner, and I don't care to ever escape. He is my prison, and his arms are the bars keeping me in place. I'm institutionalized with no hope of surviving on my own.

His lips fall from mine, working their way across my jaw and down my neck. I let my head fall back, exposing more of my throat to him. He peppers my skin with hot, scorching kisses until my shirt cuts him off, then he yanks it above my head and continues with his work, making his way to my breasts.

With his hands on my hips, I lean back until my back is against his desk. This position change gives him better access to my chest. His hands hold tight on my hips, but his mouth is free to kiss, lick, suck, and nibble. He sucks my hard nipple into his hot mouth with so much suction that it's nearly painful, but it's delightful, making every muscle tighten in anticipation. I feel a tingle forming in my stomach and know it won't take much to have me spiraling.

As if he can read my mind, his hand pushes my panties to the side and his fingers dip inside. His fingers move inside me while his thumb massages my sensitive nub. His mouth continues sucking, and before I know it, the mix of pleasure is exactly what I need to come undone. My hands, which are holding on to his shoulders, squeeze tighter, my nails are biting into his skin, and my breathing picks up as the first wave of my release hits me with unrelenting power, enough to drown me. I let out a loud moan that makes his cock stiffen against me, but his mouth and hands work harder, wanting my release.

He pushes me over the edge and I ride out every spiral, every peak, and then the fall. When my moans quiet and my body seems to relax, he pulls his hand away and removes his mouth. In one quick motion, he picks me up against him and carries me into my bedroom across the hall. He kicks the door shut behind us, then drops me onto the bed. I'm completely naked and waiting for him as I watch him undress.

I can't help but watch him move. He doesn't look like just any man getting undressed. His every move seems precise and purposeful. His hands make quick work of unbuttoning his shirt. When he pulls it away, his chest and abs are flexed with tension. His hands fall down to his jeans and he unfastens them, his biceps bulging. Finally, he pushes them down his legs and his alert cock springs free, pointing directly at me. He climbs onto the bed and seeks me out. He covers my body with his and his lips find mine again. As he kisses me, he positions himself at my entrance and pushes deep inside. Even though I just got off only moments before, finally becoming one feels like I've been starving for him—like all is finally right in the world.

I wrap my arms around his neck and hold him to me. I want him to be imprisoned too: seeing, living, and breathing nothing but me.

———

I WAKE in the morning when my alarm goes off. High tea. Great. I don't mind going, and I was even excited about getting to know his grandmother, but after last night, there's only one thing I really want to do: stay with him. Forever. I never want to part. Things felt different last night. It felt like our relationship changed, and I'm afraid the spell will break. I want him by my side always. But that's completely unreasonable and impossible. We're two different people with two different lives. We can't just lock ourselves away together and ignore the rest of the world. I'll just have to settle with the few hours a day I get with him. I roll over to find the bed empty. He's already gotten up, but I don't think much of it as I get up to shower and dress.

I exit my bedroom an hour later, dressed in a cream-colored dress that looks expensive and elegant. I complement it with a conservative pair of nude kitten heels. My hair is pulled back into a neat bun and my makeup is done softly, only bringing out my features rather than adding to them. I look around the house but he's nowhere to be found. Finally, I approach his office and knock.

"Come in," he says from the other side, and I open the door and step in.

"What do you think? Will your grandmother approve?" I ask, spinning in a circle.

He smiles as he sits back and drinks me in. "I think she will very much approve," he agrees, standing up and walking over to me.

He pulls me against his chest and kisses me.

I pull back to study his expression. "Are you okay?"

"I'm fine. Why?"

I shrug, still in his arms. "It's just you were acting a little off last night after the courier arrived, and today you left me alone in bed. You never do that."

He nods. "I just had some work that needed my attention if I'm going to be taking a couple days off."

I frown. "You're taking some days off?"

He nods. "So are you. I mean, if you're okay with that."

"Of course, but why do we need time off?"

"It's a surprise. I'm taking you away," he whispers conspiratorially.

I smile. "You are?"

He nods. "I'll give you a hint." He leans in and whispers in my ear. "Pack a bathing suit . . . a very small one. We'll be away from prying eyes for the next week—lost in our own little piece of paradise."

I smile.

He pulls back. "What do you think? Do you want to come away with me?"

"I'll go anywhere with you," I tell him, leaning in and giving him a quick kiss. "But if I'm late for tea, I have a feeling your grandmother might just break my legs . . . and a full leg cast doesn't pair well with a bikini."

H releases me and steps back, pulling out his wallet. He hands over a credit card. "After tea, go shopping for some beach clothes: bikinis, sandals, shorts. Given that you live in Chicago, I know you probably don't have a whole lot of that stuff."

"I have plenty," I argue, not wanting to spend his money.

"Well, you never did replace the things that were in that bag I threw out. So go buy yourself a new wardrobe for our trip. And don't argue. Just do it. And don't forget your passport," he says, giving me one last kiss.

I slip the card into my purse and shake my head. "Fine. What time are we leaving?"

"Our flight leaves at 7 p.m. tonight." He goes back to his desk and I turn and walk out of his office.

I can't hold back my excitement as I leave the apartment. I wonder where he's taking me. Why the surprise? Does it have anything to do with his father's call last night, followed by the hours he spent in his office? I have to admit, last night things got intense with us. It wasn't like our usual playing and fucking around. Last night seemed serious. Every time he touched my skin, I felt the power behind it. Maybe he's preparing to let me go. That would explain the intense sex and why he feels the need to take me away. It's like he's offering me one more week of pure happiness with him before he ships me back to my rundown apartment. That makes me worry, but if that's the case, I refuse to let this end badly.

Sure, it didn't start well, but things have been almost magical between us lately. I won't ruin it by refusing to say goodbye when it's time.

I finally make it to the tea room where I'm meeting his grandmother, and I'm shown to a table where she's already sitting.

"Good morning, dear," she says as I slide into my seat.

"Good morning. How are you doing?" I ask, lifting a glass of water and taking a sip.

"I'm doing very well. My body has finally adjusted to the new medication, and I feel like I could bench press a truck," she laughs out and I join in.

"Well, I'm sure you're wondering why I was so insistent on this meeting."

I smile.

"After I saw Matthew's—my Matthew, not yours—reaction to the news of the engagement, I was mortified. How shameful his behavior was." She shakes her head. "You'd think he would've figured out by now that the world doesn't revolve around him. I'm just glad I did a much better job at raising young Matthew than I did my own son." She picks up her tea and takes a sip. "I've seen Matthew turn from a man who was more like his father into a man I've become proud of, and that has everything to do with you, dear. That's a change only love can make—your love."

"Oh, I didn't do anything," I say, waving her off.

"But you did. You see, before your engagement, Matthew wasn't the man he is now. He was closed-off, stubborn, selfish. He viewed the world much like his father does. It pained me to see him turning into a bitter, jaded man at such a young age. But now, he's open, caring, giving, and in love. All of this change was brought on by you accepting his proposal."

Or by me smashing his car, but same difference, I guess.

"I'm very proud of how you've changed him by simply loving

him. I see the way he looks at you; he's never looked at another woman that way. So all this change *must* be you."

Is she right? Does he look at me differently than he did before this arrangement started? Does he love me? As I think about that question, I do a comparison in my head. How is he the same? How is he different? By the end, I know she's right. Last night was completely different than all the times before. And he didn't talk. Not once. Was he trying to tell me he loved me with actions instead of words? Is this trip meant to be something bigger?

TWENTY-TWO

MATTHEW

I have no fucking clue what I'm doing. I'm flying by the seat of my pants, hoping and praying that this works out. After last night, she has to know, right? I'll admit, I was angry when I saw the file my father had sent over. I was pissed that he would have the nerve to butt into my life like this. I was mad that he went to such great lengths to show me all the dirt he could find on her and her family. But then she knocked on my door and stepped into my office and it was like I finally saw the light. She was beautiful as she stood there with her hair dripping wet—nearly naked. I couldn't see anything you'd consider inappropriate, but it was just the thought of it lingering just out of reach that kept me going.

The moment our lips touched, I was lost. Honestly, the moment she first walked into my office, I was lost. But this is different. I'm no longer lost alone. I'm lost with her in this world we've created and I never want to leave it behind. I will make her mine, and this trip is the first step. Deep down, I think she feels like the man I've been lately is an act I'm putting on to make our little lie a little more believable. But that couldn't be further from the truth. The man I am now is a man who's finally found his soul mate—the only other person on the planet who was created just for him. The man I am now is happy, in love, and desperately clinging to something that's not supposed to be permanent. I can only hope to change her mind about me—to make her believe that the man I appear to be now is who I *am* now and will forever be. I'll never go back to living the life she saw before. And that's all because of her.

I've made plans to fly us to Brazil, where we'll get on a waiting boat so I can take her away to my grandmother's private island. The house is right on the beach, and behind it is nothing but a vast expanse of rainforest. We'll have the best of both worlds.

I've got my bags packed and I check the inside pocket of my carry-on, finding the small black box my grandmother passed on to me. It contains her engagement ring from my late grandfather. The ring itself cost nearly a million dollars, and up until she met Poppy, she'd always planned to be buried with it. Only now, she sees the love Poppy and I have for each other. She claims that Poppy's finger is the perfect spot for her ring. I only hope I can get Poppy to agree.

I've got it all planned out in my head: a romantic dinner on the porch with the ocean behind us, sun setting, dusk approaching. A delicious meal with good conversation. The two of us all alone, feeling like we're the last two people on the planet. But I'm nervous. I'm scared that the woman I've fallen in love with is only putting on a show—that she doesn't love me at all. My biggest fear is that she doesn't love me, but loathes me more than before. It's out of this fear that I've decided to wait until the last night of our vacation to ask her. I couldn't bear asking her on the first night and having her say "no," only to be awkwardly stuck together for the rest of the trip.

If she says "yes" and wants to stay longer, we'll stay as long as she'd like, but I can't risk losing her before the fun even starts. The ring is where I left it and I get to work on gathering my passport and other needed items. I'm glad our office requires all employees to have a valid passport, otherwise she wouldn't have been able to get one in time for this trip.

She makes it home at 3 p.m. on the dot and goes straight to her room to pack her bags with her new wardrobe. A little while later, she steps out and sets her bag on the floor in the living room. "I'm all packed up," she says with a small smile, handing over my credit card.

I walk over to her, placing my hands on her elbows. "How was tea?"

She shrugs. "It was fine. Weird."

"What was weird about it?"

"Your grandmother really likes me. She just kept thanking me for turning you into the man you are, who's nothing like your father, by the way." She sits on the couch and I move to sit beside her.

I let out a nervous chuckle.

"It was all good though. She seems to have high hopes for us, so this little act we're putting on must be pretty convincing."

What she says washes over me like a bucket of ice-cold water. This little act we're putting on? It hasn't been an act for me for a long time. Every day, I find myself falling more and more in love with her. I no longer want her as my fake fiancée. Now, I want her to be my wife—to share my home, my life. But I don't want to speak about it yet, so I ignore it altogether by looking at my watch. "We'd better get moving."

The two of us stand and I take our bags, leading the way to the door.

———

"BRAZIL? WE'RE IN BRAZIL?" she asks, eyes wide as she looks all around us as we're loading up in a cab.

"We are, but we're not staying in the big city. Just passing through," I tell her, taking her hand in mine.

If this were just an act, you'd think she'd pull away, given that no one we know is watching, but she doesn't. Her fingers wrap around mine as she continues to take in the sights.

We eventually make it to the boat, and I load up our bags before holding out my hand to help her down. She steps into the boat and takes her seat. I climb behind the wheel and start the engine. She looks beautiful in the early morning light. The sun is just starting to peek up over the horizon, but the stars are still lingering in the sky, holding on to every minute they have left. I get how they feel. I feel quite similar with Poppy. I'm the stars clinging to the sky as the sun threatens to push me away.

The air around us is warm and thick with moisture as we speed across the water in the direction of the island. By the time we reach it, the sun is fully out and the stars are completely gone. I shut off the boat and climb out to tie it to the dock. Then I grab our bags and her hand, pulling her up to the wooden platform.

"This is where we're staying?" she asks, looking up at the house.

"This is it. What do you think?" I ask, looking between her excited expression and the one-story house. Even though the place is old—my grandfather built it long ago—it gets minor and major renovations every year due to weather and storms that pass through.

"This is amazing. Did you rent this?"

"It belongs to my grandmother," I reply, stepping up to her side and taking her hand in mine. "My grandfather built it many, many years ago. They would come here for a month once a year. Usually the month of their anniversary. He was a real romantic—I have no idea who my father inherited his attitude from," I joke, leading her toward the house.

She stops at the end of the dock and removes her shoes, walking barefoot across the soft, pale sand. I lead her up the two steps of the porch, then we open the double glass doors.

She steps into the entryway and spins in a circle, taking it all in.

"The kitchen is to the right, obviously," I say, pointing. "This is the living room." It's big and open—nothing but floor-to-ceiling windows that show the ocean to the side of us and the green forest behind. "The bedroom and bathroom are through there," I say, pointing toward the two doors on the other side of the living room wall.

She smiles and heads for the bedroom. I follow her in, setting down our bags.

"This is amazing," she says, throwing herself back on the king-size bed.

"I'm glad you like it," I say, moving toward the bed.

I crawl up and lie by her side. She curls into me, placing one hand on my chest while her thigh rests over my hips.

"Let's just take a little nap, then we can explore," she says in a soft whisper.

I can't help but turn my head and watch as sleep takes her away. It's been a long night (and day) of traveling and it was impossible to sleep on the flight. Even though I feel tired and weak from no sleep and constant travel, I don't want to miss a minute of this. Watching her sleep in my arms feels better than heaven. It reminds me that my time with her could be limited. She could tell me "no" at the end of the week, and if she does that, I'm sure this arrangement will be over. I mean, who would want to stay with a guy who loves you when you can't stand him?

But right now, we're lost to the rest of the world and it's easy to pretend our engagement is real—that I'll get to spend the rest of my life holding her in my arms like this. I prefer the dream to real life right now. Her breathing is deep and blowing across my face. Her lips are pooched into a pout with her long lashes fanning out across the tops of her cheeks. She's beautiful and breathtaking. I only pray this isn't the end.

———

I FEEL her stir in my arms as I wake later in the day than I thought I would. I open my eyes after a couple more minutes and find her sitting on the edge of the bed. She stretches and stands up, walking to the bathroom. I lie in bed, waiting for her to return, but then I hear the sound of the shower kicking on and I get up to join her. The shower glass is already steamed up, but I can see her faint outline as she dips her head back and lets the water rush over it.

I quickly undress and step inside. Her eyes open and land on me. "I didn't mean to wake you," she says, running her fingers through her long, wet hair.

"It's okay. I don't want to miss a minute of our time here together," I reply, reaching for her. I pull her to my chest and cup her cheek. Staring into her dark eyes, I lean in and kiss her gently, softly. She kisses me back and pulls away with a smile.

"What's the plan for the day? Is there anything specific you want to do?"

I shrug. "We can do whatever you want. We could go back to the mainland and see the sights. We could spend the day on the beach— listening to music and drinking. We could just take it easy today, have dinner, and get a good night's sleep to prepare for tomorrow. It's up to you. There's no agenda on this trip."

She begins washing off. "I think a beach day sounds good. Do we have the stuff to make those cute frozen drinks?"

"I'm sure we have some tequila and mix. A margarita beach day it is."

"Don't make them too strong though. You know how well I hold my liquor."

I laugh. "Virgin margaritas for you then."

"No, I would like to just chill and relax, so a *little* tequila."

I nod in agreement. "Okay. I'll go make a pitcher. You get that bikini on."

I step out of the shower without washing off, because if we're going to spend the day all sweaty and lying in the sun, then what's the point in showering? I wrap my towel around my waist and go to the bedroom to pull on some swim shorts. I head into the kitchen, make our margaritas, then look through the fully stocked fridge to assemble a snack tray.

I hear the back door open, and when I carry everything out, she's already outside, setting up the lounge chairs. My eyes find her bikini body and I nearly trip over my own two feet.

She looks up at me and laughs. "Been walking long?"

"I suddenly forget how to do a lot of things when I see this much of your skin," I reply, setting everything down on the table between us.

We each take our seats and I hand her a frozen margarita. I watch as she takes a sip. She seems pleasantly surprised and takes another.

"This is good. I can't even taste the alcohol. Dangerous." She winks.

"I'm glad you like it," I say, sitting back in my seat. I pull out my phone and get some music playing, but turn it down so it's more background noise than anything else. I turn my head to see her place her drink on the table. Then she scoots down in her lounge chair until she's lying back, relaxed. Her eyes close as she absorbs the sun. I can't stop myself from taking her in—from her white painted toes to her long legs to her flat stomach and full, perky tits. I've already memorized the curve of her hips, the dip in her spine, and the swell of her breasts. I know her body better than I know my own, and that gives me a little bit of solace when I consider how this could all end up.

The two of us sunbathe for an hour while we listen to music and have our drinks. With the sun still so high in the sky, my body is hot and sweaty. "Want to take a swim?" I ask.

Her smile lights up her face. "Yes, I'm burning up." She stands and sways on her feet, but I quickly reach out and steady her.

I laugh. "Hasn't anyone ever told you not to stand after drinking and sitting down for so long?"

"I wasn't sitting down; I was lying down. I'm fine." She pushes my hands away and rushes toward the water. She runs until it's deep enough, then she sails through the air and dives in deeper. I wade in, watching her swim underwater until she pops up.

"This is perfect. It's almost like bathwater." She pushes her wet hair away from her face.

"It does feel pretty good," I agree, swimming over to her and pulling her against my chest. She wraps her arms and legs around me.

"It's beautiful here. Thank you for bringing me. I never could've imagined a place like this. This is my first time leaving the country. Glad I finally got to use my passport!"

"You deserve it," I say, leaning in and kissing her jaw.

"I wish I could stay here forever."

I laugh. "What would you do?"

She shrugs. "I don't know. I mean, if real life weren't a thing and I didn't have to work and pay bills and all that, I'd just read, learn piano, swim, and maybe take up painting or something. Just enjoy life instead of always worrying how I'll be able to pay for this or manage that, you know?"

"Wouldn't you miss real life though? I mean, wouldn't you eventually want to get married, have children?"

"I can do that here. Raise children on the island. I could homeschool them and keep them shielded from the real world," she says around a laugh.

"If you never leave the island, then how are you going to find someone to have those kids with?"

"Oh. Good point." Her eyes move up as she thinks it over. "Would you mind donating some sperm?" She laughs.

"You want my children?" I ask as a flash flood of emotion fills my body.

"Are we having the 'future kids' talk?" she asks, drawing her brows together.

I shrug. "I guess we are. You know, hypothetically."

She nods. "Well then, yes. I would love to have your children one day."

"How many?"

"In an ideal world, two. A boy and a girl. Who needs more than one of each?"

I laugh. "I like the sound of that," I agree, moving back in to press my lips to hers.

TWENTY-THREE

POPPY

This place is magical and amazing. Even though I know I shouldn't allow myself to think this way, I can't help but pretend that Matthew and I are actually an engaged-to-be-married couple. I like to think about how our lives could play out . . . getting married, having children, growing old together, and coming here every year for some time away sounds perfect and romantic. Being here alone with him makes those dreams feel as if they're almost possible. There's no one to put on a show for in Brazil, but there's no reason to pump the brakes either—not when he's pulling me against him, kissing me, touching me, loving me—even if it isn't real love.

We spend our first day lounging on the beach, drinking margaritas, and eating exotic local fruits and vegetables I've never even heard of. The sun is high and warm, the sky a cloudless blue. The smooth, calm water shimmers and dances like millions of tiny crystals. The sand is white and feels like baby powder beneath my feet, like I'm walking on a cloud in heaven. This place is that perfect. It *could* be heaven.

When the sun starts to descend in the sky, we make our way inside to prepare dinner. The two of us seem to be perfectly in sync here. When he moves, I move, and when I reach, he walks into my arms without me having to say a word. It almost feels like this was meant to be—like this game we started was perfectly planned out. But who in the world could've seen this coming? I never thought I'd be so desperately in love with anyone—let alone him. It almost hurts to breathe, knowing that each breath with him is limited. I'm hyper-aware of each heartbeat, knowing that with each one, that's only another second of time with him I'll never get back.

I know I shouldn't think this way, but I can't help but feel like this is our last week together—that this is my big send-off. He's giving me one final, perfect week with him. Next week, everything goes back to normal—like a dream fading away with the early morning light. I know it's not fair to feel sad, because I've gotten more from him than I ever thought I would, but I want more. So much more.

The two of us have dinner and I push my sadness away. I wish this were real, and I try to make myself believe it is, even if only to keep the sadness at bay until it's time for it to be felt. We laugh and talk over dinner and it seems like he finds any excuse to touch me. That confuses me, because I don't know if he's trying to get in as many touches as he can before we end, or if it's because he really is that drawn to me. It's easier for me to believe that this is it—that he's tired of our game but wants it to end nicely. Maybe he doesn't think I could love him. Perhaps he feels I'm the one playing nice just to avoid a felony and possible jail time.

After cleaning up following dinner, we shower together—again—and he's always touching me. Then we fall into bed, completely wrapped up in each other, only to sleep and start another new day. I count the minutes we have left and pray for more.

The week passes by quickly—too quickly. We've spent every second of our time together touring the mainland, hiking the rain-forest behind the house, swimming in the ocean, and lounging on the beach. At night, we come together in the way we do best. But today is our last day here. Tomorrow we leave bright and early to make our 10 a.m. flight home, back to normal life.

I haven't brought up anything I found out at high tea, not waiting to ruin our time here. But all the questions are on the tip of my tongue and they're burning to be released. Still, I refuse to go there until it's time.

We prepare dinner together. I pour us each a glass of wine and we take everything out to the patio table. The sound of the waves crashing is like music at this point—perfect and speaking a language few know and can understand. But I understand. It's like all the secrets and questions inside of me: loud, unstoppable, dying to be heard.

He sits across from me at the table with a candle burning between us. He cuts into his chicken and takes a bite while I have a sip of wine.

"Have you enjoyed yourself?" he asks.

"I'm kind of sad to leave, to be honest. I love this place." I look around at all the beauty this little island has to offer and wish I could stay here forever.

He chuckles. "I'll have to bring you back sometime."

It's easy to read into that statement. I wish it meant we'd spend our lives together and come back here every year like his grandparents did, but I'm sure it's more of a polite statement than anything else.

"I'd love that," I reply, feeling my heart crack.

"When we get back home, your piano lessons will start."

"When we get back home?" I ask, feeling my brow furrow.

He looks up, confused. "You're not really planning on staying on the island, are you?" he asks with an amused expression.

I laugh. "No, but . . ." I let my words fall away. To me, they may as well have fallen into the sand for the ocean to carry them away.

"What is it?" he asks, taking my hand and looking at me with those dark brown eyes.

I wet my lips, unsure if I should say anything. I don't want to ruin our time here. "It's just that I was thinking this was it."

"What's it?" he asks, still not catching on.

"I talked with your grandmother . . . I know she's fine, Matthew. She's not dying." I didn't want to spill everything like this, but now I feel like he's just torturing me—dragging things out and giving me false hope. "I don't know if you made all that up or if they've magically found a way to cure whatever illness she had, but there's no point to the game anymore. If I'm being honest, I've just been going along with it because I've been enjoying it so much."

His face goes slack, understanding. "You talked to my grandmother?"

I nod. "At tea. I know you said not to bring up her health, but *she* brought it up. And she made it seem like she plans on being here for a really long time—talking about helping with our wedding plans and watching our children grow up. Then I asked if she really thought all that was possible and she looked confused. She made it very clear that she's as healthy as a horse."

He lets out a deep chuckle.

"What's so funny?" I wait, but he continues to laugh. "This isn't funny! My feelings, emotions, and wasted time aren't funny! We either have to break up or really get married, Matthew. Your grandmother is fine."

"I know she's fine," he laughs out.

I freeze. "What do you mean? Did she call you? When did you plan on telling me?"

"Don't be mad," he says, holding up his hand as he gets control over his laughing.

I sit, waiting patiently for his explanation.

"I lied about my grandmother. She isn't dying. I made it up. It was the only thing I could think of to get you to agree to our arrangement," he confesses.

He lied about the whole thing? Why? "Why would you do that?"

He shrugs and takes a deep breath. "I wanted you, Poppy. From the moment you first walked into my office for your interview in that pencil skirt and those red heels, I wanted you. But it was like from the moment I opened my mouth, you hated me. And then, I hated you . .

. but I only hated you because you hated me, and I knew that I'd never get my chance with you. I was angry at myself because you hated me so badly. I hated myself for not being the type of guy you could see yourself with. I hated you because even though I have a good job and money and my shit together, that I still wasn't good enough for you. So, yes, I lied. I tricked you so I could give myself what I wanted, no matter how you felt about it."

I'm not even sure what to say to that. Should I be angry? Should I feel sorry for him? Should I be happy that he did what he did in order to get me to where I am now? I can't help but feel a little bit of every-thing. He lied and tricked me. He manipulated me to satisfy his own needs, though if I'm honest, so did I. I purposefully tried to make him hate me to fire me, dump me, and let me get away with assaulting his car. I can't deny the fact that we both completely fucked this whole thing up, but instead of hatred or anger, I realize I still love him more than anything.

I don't even know how to address this, so I let out a long breath and join his laughter. "So what's the plan now? Your grandmother isn't dying and your whole family thinks we're engaged. Where do we go from here? What was your endgame?"

"Well, actually," he says, pulling a black box from his pocket, "this is my grandmother's ring. It's been in our family for hundreds of years—passed down time and time again."

My mouth drops open and I freeze.

"I know I wasn't honorable in how I got you here, but I feel like everything between us happened for a reason. You're my reason to live now, Poppy, and I'm sorry I had to take the steps I did to get us here. If I only could have been this man when we met, things may have gone differently. But the man I am now isn't an act. I'm not trying to fool you or anyone into thinking I'm something other than what I am. I'm this person because of you. Being with you, touching you, kissing you, falling in love with you—it's all made me who I am today. And I can't thank you enough for that. I never thought when I started this whole thing that this is how we'd end up, but I can't help but feel like things happened for a reason. I don't want to lose you. I thought one night of having you in my bed would be enough. But it's not. I can't settle for anything less than having you in my arms every single night for the rest of my life. One night with you—hell, one month or year with you—would never be enough. I need forever. Will you marry me . . . for real this time?"

He opens the box and my mouth drops open wide. I take in the ring and it's far better than the pretend engagement ring he purchased before. This ring is *huge!* One massive diamond in the center with dozens of little ones surrounding it. The band is gold and shining like it's never even been worn. It's beautiful and breathtaking and exciting. But what do I say?

I've been so focused on our ending that I never even imagined that this could happen. I thought my feelings were one-sided and that his were nothing more than an act. But I was wrong. So wrong. He loves me!

TWENTY-FOUR

MATTHEW

Time has stopped. Everything is frozen in this moment as I watch her stare at the ring with her eyes wide and mouth hanging open. I have no idea what's going through her head, and that scares the living shit out of me. This whole week—this whole month —has been leading up to this one moment. I think my heart and lungs stop working as I anxiously await her answer.

I can't say I'd blame her for turning me down—not after the lies and manipulation I used to get her here—but I can only pray she sees past that. That was a desperate act from an even more desperate man. I did whatever I needed to do to get her here, and as much as I hate the way I did it, I could never regret it.

"Poppy," I say her name and her eyes pop up to lock on mine. "Will you marry me?"

She shakes her head, her mouth still hanging open. "I . . . I don't know."

"Do you love me?" I ask, leveling my eyes on her.

Her mouth closes and her eyes fill with tears as she nods her head.

I breathe a sigh of relief. "I love you too, and I need to know that you're mine for the rest of my life." I get up and walk around the table to her side, falling down on one knee, still presenting the ring to her. "I need you by my side. I need you every day for the rest of my life. I will spend my life proving to you day after day that I'm the man you helped me become—that I'm the man you've fallen in love with. Will you please, *please* marry me?" My eyes fall closed, anxiously waiting.

There's a long pause as she thinks, and I refuse to open my eyes for fear of seeing the word NO stamped all over her face. If she says "no," I don't know what I'll do or how I'll move on. I've never been in love before—not like this. I don't know how to heal from heartbreak. My best guess is that I wouldn't. I'll never recover if I lose her.

"Yes," she breathes out. She said it so softly that I almost didn't catch it.

My eyes pop open to study her face. There are still unshed tears in her eyes, but she's wearing a soft smile.

"Yes," she says again, a little louder this time.

My own smile breaks free and I take off the pretend engagement ring and replace it with the real one. I pull her into my arms and kiss her. I kiss her until I can't breathe anymore, and then I continue to kiss her. I don't need air if I have her.

I plant both knees on the deck and pull her against me, falling back to sit with my legs stretched out and her sitting on top of me. Her arms are around my neck as she kisses me in a way she's never kissed me before. She was holding out before, because now I can feel every ounce of love she has for me. It's pouring out of her and raining down on me like I've been trapped in a tropical storm without any shelter. She is the storm. My storm.

Dinner has been completely forgotten as I push myself up with her in my arms. I carry her into the house, but my need to be inside her now is too great to make it all the way to the bedroom. I press her back against the wall right inside the door I didn't care enough to close. My hands move up her loose skirt and find her panties. With one firm yank, they're ripped and falling to the floor. I reach between us, freeing myself from my shorts. Only seconds later, I'm sliding deep into her core.

She lets out a sound of both joy and relief, and it makes my cock twitch inside her. Her heat and tightness welcome me—almost scorching me, but in a painless way. It's overwhelmingly perfect in every single way possible. Our kiss hasn't broken, but I think I've finally learned to live without air, because the burn in my lungs is now gone, replaced with euphoric tingles that take over my whole body.

As her muscles tighten around me and her whimpers and moans grow louder, I lose myself in her storm as it rains down on me so heavily that I can't see anything past her. But that's okay. As long as I have her, I don't need to see anything else anyway.

———

WE MAKE IT BACK HOME, but that doesn't change anything between us. We're a newly engaged couple who can't keep their hands to themselves. The moment we walk in, she's back in my arms and I'm carrying her over to the piano. Time to break it in properly.

Minutes turn into hours, and hours into days. Neither of us has escaped our own little world to go back out into society. Our time is spent making love, sleeping, and repeating the process. We've been home for two days but haven't even left the house. In here, we're perfect. In here, nothing can get to us. But tomorrow we'll finally have to return to work, and I hate the thought of venturing out into the real world. I much prefer the one we've created. Despite it all, we dress to go over to my grandmother's for our rescheduled dinner, since we missed Friday night due to our vacation.

Even though I don't want to leave the apartment, I'm excited to see the look on Gran's face when she sees that Poppy has accepted the ring.

We walk into her house and we're told to go out to the patio rather than the lounge, which I find odd, but I lead Poppy out with a smile. I stop when I walk out and find not only my Gran, but my father too, along with a young woman who looks like she's paid by the hour, if you know what I mean. She has long, blonde hair—the unnatural kind—overdone makeup, and a tight dress I'm sure has my grandmother in a tizzy.

"Oh, hello," I say, looking at my father and ignoring the escort who's clearly being paid to be here. "I wasn't expecting to see you here," I say, pulling Poppy up to my side.

He unfolds his hands and gestures for us to sit down. "I know. I wasn't sure if I could make it, but here I am."

Gran looks up at Poppy and smiles. "It's nice to see you again, dear."

Poppy gives her a quick hug before taking a seat.

"I see that you've accepted my ring." She smiles. "That's wonderful."

Poppy looks down at the ring on her finger with a smile and nods. "It really is. I love it, but are you sure you don't want to hang on to it? It's so beautiful and has so much history."

"Nonsense. That's been passed down for generations, and right there on your hand is where it belongs now. I have high hopes for the two of you."

"I do too, Gran," I agree, wrapping my arm around Poppy while I take the drink the maid is offering.

I hand Poppy the glass and take another for myself.

"Matthew, son, I'd like to introduce you to Bethany. Bethany is the daughter of Roger Steinbeck. You remember him, don't you?"

I think back, trying to figure out who Roger Steinbeck is. "Should I?" I ask, raising my glass to my lips but freezing.

He almost rolls his eyes but refrains. "Roger is in line to take over the company. I'm retiring soon. He's taking the spot that was meant for you."

"That's nice, Dad," I reply, looking over at my grandmother. "So, how've you been, Gran?"

She smiles but she knows my father isn't done, so she doesn't reply.

"Matthew," my father says, leaning forward slightly.

Resentfully, I look back at him.

"I brought Bethany here to meet you. To show you that you have so many more options than what you think you have."

Poppy's mouth drops. She know this is clearly about her, and after that file he sent me, I should have expected something like this.

"I know my options, Dad, and I'm more than happy with the choice I've made." I reach over, placing my hand on Poppy's knee.

His dark, beady eyes watch as my hand moves to rest on her leg. His back straightens and his eyes narrow. Finally, he looks over at Gran. "How could you give her that ring?"

Gran seems surprised that her son would be so rude. I, however, am not. "That was my decision and none of your business," she replies.

"None of my business?" he asks, running a hand through his thick black-and-gray hair. "That was a family heirloom, and you've just given it away to a gold digger." His eyes flash toward Poppy before bouncing back to Gran.

Poppy stands up. "I am not a gold digger!"

Dad looks up at her, surprised that she would actually stick up for herself. He rolls his eyes, annoyed that he seems to have upset this woman he considered to be so far beneath him. "Look, honey, I didn't mean for you to take offense. It's just that you have to see the striking difference between the two of you. There are certain expectations when you're a Lewis. It's nothing personal."

She gasps and I stand up to defend her, but Gran speaks above us all.

"Matthew Lewis!" she shouts, and I jump to attention even though I know I'm not the Matthew in trouble. "I will not sit by and watch you devastate this girl. She is a very good woman who may not have come from money, but she makes up for that in compassion and kindness. Something you have none of. It wouldn't hurt you to take a lesson from her. Now, this is my house and I will not tolerate your tone any longer. If you can't control yourself, you know where the door is. If you leave, please do not return until you know how to be civilized. This family may have money, but we also have class, and I've got serious doubts about you. This young lady, however, belongs more than you do in this moment. I'm closing this discussion for good." Her eyes look from my father to me, then soften when she looks at Poppy, but then they take on a harder edge when she looks back at my father.

Dad looks from her, to me, to Poppy, and then back. It's like he's trying to decide what he should do. He didn't expect Gran to jump to her rescue. Right now, it's three against one. He's outnumbered and he's always been a man of numbers. He knows when he's lost, but he's not a good loser. He's a spoiled child who's ready to throw a tantrum the moment he's denied something he wants.

"So this is how it's going to be?' he asks, looking only at her. "You're choosing her over your own son?"

"I'm not choosing anyone, dear. I simply prefer to be in the company of those I can enjoy, and your company is less than favorable," Gran replies.

Dad lets out a long breath, shakes his head, then pushes himself forward, the girl quickly following along.

"Matthew, please show your father out. We still have class, after all."

I do as I'm asked, following them to the door, but there are a million things on the tip of my tongue I'm trying to hold back.

TWENTY-FIVE

POPPY

"Poppy," Matthew's grandmother says once we're left alone on the patio. I look up to meet her eyes and she continues, "I don't want anything that was said here tonight to sway your decision. I was just like you once."

"You were?" I ask, already filled with doubt about this marriage.

She nods. "I didn't come from money. In fact, when I married my late husband, I didn't have any money to my name at all. I was living with my parents who were hard-working but very poor. Matthew, my husband, was the one who came from money, and I had to fight with his family, just like you're doing now. They said I was trash—that I didn't belong in their world, and that our marriage would never work. Well," she smiles, "here I am, nearly six decades later."

"Did they ever accept you?"

"I don't think so. Though it got to a point where they no longer cared. I dreaded every holiday with a passion, because I knew it meant I had to be around them. But after the first few months of our marriage, they began to hold their tongues. Instead of offending me with their words, they ignored me. And to me, being ignored was better than the constant fighting. When his father passed away, his mother only grew to be more bitter. And when she passed away, I helped to organize her funeral." She smiles. "I put her in this god-awful gown and mismatched shoes. I remember her wearing the gown once. She did nothing but complain about how uncomfortable it was—how it looked to be made out of some middle-class house's drapes. But she had to wear it once, because it was a gift from her husband. So I picked the most hideous thing in her closet, and that's what she's buried in—still wearing to this day," she says with a content smile and a head nod.

I can't hold back my laugh.

"I realize it was petty of me, but damn, did it feel good in the moment!" She lets out a long laugh now and I join in. "So, see, everything comes full circle and works itself out. I can only hope that we have a better relationship than I had with my mother-in-law, and that you respect my wishes."

"After that, how could I not?" I laugh out.

"The point, dear, is that you will always be welcome in my home. Please don't let one bad apple ruin your life for you. You two are good for each other. Don't let anything get in the way of what you have."

I nod, letting her know I've heard her words, then Matthew walks back to the patio and takes my hand in his.

"Are you all right?" he asks, leaning in like he doesn't even care his grandmother is watching us so intently.

"I'm fine," I promise.

"Are you sure? I'm sorry about my father. He's always been an asshole." He freezes like he's just realized he's done something he shouldn't. "Sorry about the language, Gran."

"Asshole is an understatement," she replies, causing all of us to laugh.

The rest of dinner progresses without a hitch. We talk, laugh, eat, and drink expensive wine. By the time we leave, I feel almost giddy, and I've completely forgotten about our before-dinner drinks and the conversation that took place. Matthew and I load back up into the car and he starts the drive home. He seems tense, though, probably still annoyed by his father, so I want to break the ice.

"Did you know that your grandmother and great-grandmother didn't get along?"

He looks over at me quickly. "No. Did she tell you that?"

I nod. "She said she didn't come from money, so when she started seeing your grandfather, his family did not approve—they made her life hell, basically."

"Huh," he replies.

"She said they never did accept her. Instead, they switched from pulling stunts like your father did to just ignoring her altogether."

He lets out a long breath. "I just hope that isn't how our lives go."

"She said that when she buried your great-grandmother, she put her in a dress she hated, with mismatched shoes to boot," I laugh out the last bit and he joins in.

The cab of the car is no longer filled with thick tension. Now that it's full of our laughter, everything else falls away.

"That does sound like my Gran. She's feisty. Just like you." He squeezes my hand.

We ride the rest of the way home in silence. I'm too lost in thought to think up something to talk about. I wonder if my life will be anything like his grandmother's. Obviously, I won't have to deal with his whole family hating me—just his father. But can I deal with that? Going to family parties and being treated like an outcast the whole time? Will every family event be filled with drama? Our wedding? The births of our children if we have any? Every Christmas, Thanksgiving, birthday party? Is Matthew worth that?

We make it home, and once we're inside, we go directly to our rooms to get ready for bed. I take my time in removing my jewelry and showering, just wanting more time alone to think. I never thought Matthew and I would end up here: in love and ready to get married, with this father threatening to tear us apart at any moment.

I'm brushing my hair when I hear my bedroom door open. Matthew walks in shirtless, muscles flexing as he walks over to me. He steps up behind me and presses a kiss to my shoulder.

"What are you thinking about?"

I set my brush down and spin around to face him. "Your father," I confess.

He shakes his head. "Don't. Don't give him any more energy than he deserves. Don't let him tear us apart." His hands find my hips and he pulls me closer. I rest my head against his chest. "He's taken so much from me already. Don't let him take you too," he whispers, pressing a kiss to my head.

And that's when I decide. He's right. I never cared about what people thought of me before. Why am I letting it affect me now? I'm happy with Matthew. I love him and he loves me. Why shouldn't we get what we both want?

"No one is taking me away from you," I reply, lifting my head from his chest to look up at him. Our eyes lock and something is exchanged. Honesty. Truth. Love.

I reach around his neck and pull his mouth to mine. He kisses me softly and slowly, full of love and relief—relief that I'm not running.

He picks me up against him. "Come on. Let's go to bed," he says, carrying me out of my bathroom, down the hall, and into his room where we stay for the rest of the night.

———

AFTER THAT, things return to normal. We go to work, then we come home every night to be together, even though we each have our own things to do. I've finished my etiquette classes, which were mostly pointless, but at least I now know which fork to use during each course of a fancy dinner. I also have my piano lessons and my personal trainer. Matthew has changed his workout schedule around so we're both at the gym at the same time. This gives us more time together outside of the gym too. Every Friday night, we go to his grandmother's house for dinner, but his father hasn't shown his face again.

Matthew says his father has always gotten everything he's ever wanted. But he didn't get what he wanted this time, so he's off sulking. He bets he won't show his face at dinner again for a long time.

Sunday mornings, the three of us have brunch. Once a month, we switch it up and enjoy high tea. I'm really connecting with his grandmother in ways I never expected to. She tells me stories about Matthew as a child and the trouble he'd get into. She tells me things about the family—people I've never met. She also tells me stories from her youth: how she grew up, the things she did, the men she'd been with. It's like diving into an old history book that's more personal—not just facts, but opinions too. I truly enjoy every minute I get to spend with her, and the funny thing is, I find myself wanting to call her throughout the day like she's my best friend. I don't want to bother her though, so I usually just make a mental note of things to talk about the next time we see her.

Time passes quickly and perfectly. Locked away at home, we always felt like nothing could ever get to us, but now, nothing can get to us out there either. We're together forever. I almost feel like I'm living a real-life version of the *Cinderella* story—a poor girl who never had anyone finally finds her Prince Charming. And although life isn't perfect and Matthew and I still have our squabbles from time to time, we always overcome it with laughter and love.

———

MONTHS PASS and our wedding preparations begin. We hire a wedding planner and find a location. We opt for a destination wedding at his grandmother's private island. I never saw myself getting married on the beach, but it seems fitting considering how he proposed. And honestly, I can't wait to go back. The ceremony will be private—only close friends and family. And all their expenses are paid, including the hotel we're renting for them to stay in after the festivities are done. I don't think anyone has ever invited everyone to their honeymoon location then sent them away instead of leaving them behind, but I like the backwardness of it all. Not to mention, Chicago is booked solid for years to come. It's like if you want a nice venue in Chicago, you have to book it when you're born. I didn't want the stress of it all. This seemed like the best and easiest option.

Now the countdown begins. The wedding planner is handling every aspect for me after I gave her full control, not caring about any of the details as long as he and I are together. My only job is to find a dress and show up. Matthew knows I'm not much of a shopper, so instead of sending me out with a credit card in hand, he arranges for someone to bring racks and racks of dresses to me in the privacy of our own home. He promises to stay in his office so he doesn't see the dress before the big day.

Someone knocks on the door and I answer it, watching and laughing as he rushes to his office to get out of the way. The moment I open the door, people are lined up outside in the hallway, and they begin pushing in rack after rack. I stand back, watching in awe as the living room transforms into a bridal store.

With a deep breath, I start going through the dresses. When I find one I like, I hang it on an empty rack. Each time I'm done going through a rack, someone wheels it out. Slowly but surely, I manage to get everything down to one rack—the one that has every dress I like. There are only 10 dresses on it, and even that seems overwhelming. The men leave the room and the women stay to help me dress. There's a long fold-out mirror against the wall and another behind me, so I can see every angle of the dresses I try on.

The first one is too much—too puffy, too glittery. It's pretty, but not timeless and not meant to see sand and ocean water. I take it off and they take it away, bringing in another dress. I never thought I'd be a bridezilla, but I manage to find something wrong with every dress I'd picked out. Every single one . . . except one. The last one. I put it on and it's made of a crisp white statin material. It's thin and form-fitting. The sleeves are small, only hanging off my shoulders instead of sitting on them, and the back is cut low, almost to my ass. It hugs my breasts, dipping low between them and giving just enough of a peek to be sexy, but not enough to look overdone. It fits my upper body like a second skin, but it flows down to my feet in a soft flare. It doesn't have a massively long train either. It's simple. Elegant. Timeless. I know when I look back at pictures of me in this dress, I won't think, "Oh my God, what was I thinking?" And that's the most important part.

When all the dresses are gone, I go into his office and he looks up at me with surprise.

"Did you find something you liked?"

I nod and smile. "I did. I think you'll love it."

He smiles wide. "I'll love anything you choose."

I slip into his lap. "What have you been doing in here?"

"Oh, just going over some files. Hey, there's an event we've been invited to this weekend. I thought it would be nice to get our minds off the wedding for a while and just have fun. What do you think?" He looks up at me, hopeful.

"What kind of event is it?" I ask, unsure.

"It's just an engagement party for an old friend."

"So your father won't be there?" I ask.

He frowns. "I'm not sure. He may be there. It's sort of a mutual friend, but we can't let him dictate our lives. If there's something we want to do, we should do it without a second thought."

I let out a long breath. "I don't know, Matthew. I'm just worried that something will be said and a fight will break out, ruining the party."

"My father is nothing but polite in public. I promise he won't say anything about us if other people are around. Come on. What do you say?" he asks, shaking me against his chest in a playful way.

I can't help but laugh. His smile is infectious. "All right. I'll go."

"Good! You'll need a dress."

"Oh no. Not that again."

He chuckles. "I'll order one for you. You won't have to do anything but put it on."

"Now you're talking my language," I laugh out.

TWENTY-SIX

MATTHEW

The weekend quickly approaches, as it always does when I'm spending time with her. I'm actually looking forward to this party. It's been a long time since I saw and hung out with the guys I grew up with, and for once, I feel like my life is going according to plan. Before, I'd avoid these type of things, not wanting to show up because everyone but me would be talking about their amazing life. But finally, my life *is* great. I have a beautiful woman on my arm who's about to be my wife, and we're about to start a wonderful life together. I have nothing to hide.

I dress in my tux and slick back my hair, applying a squirt of cologne before exiting my room. I expect to find Poppy already waiting for me, but I should've guessed she'd be having problems with the dress. I walk down the hall and knock on her door. "Poppy, you about ready?"

"Can you zip me up?" she asks from the other side.

I open the door and step inside, finding her spinning in circles like a dog chasing its tail. I laugh as I step up to her and she stops spinning. I place my hand on the zipper at her lower back and pull it up. The dress zips up perfectly and smoothly, just like I knew it would.

"I do have an eye for dress sizes," I say, leaning in and kissing her neck.

She blushes. "I don't know if that's a good thing or a bad thing."

I let my eyes rake up and down her body, taking her in. It's a black dress that hugs her body and curves to perfection. It's sleeveless and has a plunging neckline. The back is open, sexy.

"Looking at you now, I'd say it's a good thing," I reply, holding out my elbow. She takes it and I lead her out of the room and to the door. "I've hired a limo for us tonight. I thought it would be appropriate for the occasion."

"A limo? That sounds pretty fancy."

"Well, where we're going is fancy, hence the formal dress," I remind her.

We make it downstairs and outside to where the limo is waiting. The driver sees us coming and opens the back door. I allow her to slide in first, then climb in behind her. The door is shut and we're surrounded in darkness, only lit by the soft running lights along the top.

"Would you like some champagne?"

"I'd love some. Thank you," she replies. I pop the bottle and pour some into both glasses.

I hand her glass over and she takes the tiniest of sips. She's still not big on drinking, but in my world, alcohol is everywhere—at every dinner, every party. So she's come around to the taste and she can hold a glass or two.

"This is amazing," she says, looking around.

"First time in a limo?"

"Yes and no. It's my first time in this type of limo. A bunch of friends rented a stretch Hummer once to drive us from bar to bar. It was cool, but this is elegant and fancy." She looks over at me and I see the darkness in her eyes. I lean in and kiss her, and she isn't greedy. She gives me everything in this kiss.

"I should rent us a limo more often," I say, more to myself.

She giggles but lets the subject drop as we enjoy our champagne and get closer to the venue.

"Where are we going anyway?"

"Chez Wedding Venue," I reply. "Very upscale and fancy. The more I think about it, the happier I am that you chose the island for our wedding."

She smiles. "I think it's perfect for us."

"I agree."

Soon we're standing in a massive all-white room that's decorated beautifully. There's a big staircase with glass railings and flowers along every step. Tables are set up with white tablecloths, big bouquets in the center, and hundreds of little lights hanging every-where. Everything is beautiful, fancy, and rich.

"Would you like to get something to eat?" I ask as we're walking by the buffet-style dinner table.

"I'm fine for now, thank you," she replies, walking alongside me.

I introduce her to a few family friends and everything is fine. But then we notice my father, and I can feel her back stiffen beside me. He sees us as he's talking with a group of friends, and he says some-thing I can't hear given how far away we are, but then he heads in our direction.

"He's coming over here," she whispers.

"Just brace yourself. He won't say anything out of line tonight."

We stand, waiting for my father to approach. He finally does as he offers me a handshake. "Matthew, how have you been?" he asks very formally.

"I'm well. And yourself?"

He nods curtly. "Very well. I'm glad to see you could make it. The Rich family means a lot to me and the family."

"I wouldn't have missed it." I look around. "I'm surprised Gran isn't here."

"Oh, well, you know how she is. She's avoiding me and every-thing I may attend." He tips up his glass and takes a swig. "Anyway, carry on." He walks off and I feel Poppy let out a long breath she must have been holding.

"Let's dance," I say, pulling her to the dance floor.

I spin her around so she lands softly against my chest, and I hold her close as I begin to lead.

"That's a relief," she breathes out.

"Nah, it's all about who's around to witness. And my father is not a fan of witnesses. He couldn't *not* address me. Then the rumor mill would churn with possible family drama. He can't have anyone thinking that."

She shakes her head. "I can't even begin to understand how someone can live a life worrying about other people's opinions, or how someone can try so hard to keep up appearances."

"Welcome to the life I grew up in," I respond.

She lets the conversation drop as we dance, and I can tell she isn't comfortable here, but I keep trying to get her to forget everyone else and just focus on having a good time with me like we always do.

After we dance, we find a table to rest at for a bit. A few more people come over to talk, including my father's old friend, Jefferson, and his new, young wife, Tabitha. Jefferson is my father's age. Tabitha's around 21. Yeah, that's a gold digger if I ever saw one. But I don't point it out. I just keep up with the conversation, keeping things light. Nothing serious is discussed, as is the norm at these types of parties. Poppy and Tabitha sit and chat a while and they seem to be hitting it off. I hear a few giggles and laughs as I talk with Jefferson.

When the couple leaves, Poppy excuses herself to use the restroom, leaving me alone. I hope she hurries, because I fear having to talk to one of my exes since a couple of them are also in attendance. While she's gone, I focus on enjoying my drink while taking in the party, looking at faces, and trying to remember why I ever tried so hard to be a part of this world. I haven't done this type of thing in years, and now I'm suddenly seeing why. I try to look at everything from Poppy's point of view as an outsider. People wear fake smiles, fake laugh, and pretend everything's perfect. I could point out 10 guys right now who are having affairs on the wives who are on their arms, pretending their whole life is perfect. Now more than ever, I want nothing to do with these people. I want to live a normal life—a happy life where I come home every night to the woman I love. I want happy children who feel like they have it all because they have two parents who love them.

I'm far past my limit of pretenses for the evening, so as soon as Poppy exits the restroom, I'm taking her home where we can get started on *that* life, not this one.

My father comes up to me and pats me on the shoulder. "Come with me," he says.

"Dad, I'm just about to head out. I don't have time for this."

He stops walking away and spins around to face me. "Matthew, there is someone here I'd like to introduce you to. Please, come with me."

To keep from making a scene, I get up and follow him over to a group of men. "Gentlemen, this is my son, Matthew Lewis III." He smiles proudly. "Matthew, these are my old college buddies, Frank, Jim, Barry, and Justin Burns."

Justin Burns? That's a name I recognize. "It's a pleasure to meet you all," I say, moving in to shake their hands.

"We've heard a lot about you," one of the men says. "You sure do make your father proud."

I let out a bitter laugh. "I doubt that."

My father places his hand on my shoulder. "Now, son, don't be modest. I'm very proud of you and what you do. I'm sure it's only a matter of time before you're opening your own law office."

"Well, you've invested in his business, I'm sure," another guy says.

"Of course. He knows as soon as he's ready for that next step, he doesn't have to go to anyone but me," Dad gushes like he wasn't just telling me my soon-to-be wife wasn't good enough.

I can't just stand here and take these lies built upon lies. I can't even keep them straight anymore. "Excuse me, gentlemen, but I must go. Please carry on," I say, interrupting their talk. Dad gives me an angry scowl, but I turn my back on him like he's done to me so many times. I walk away, looking for Poppy. I was wrong to bring her here. I don't know why I didn't see it before.

TWENTY-SEVEN

POPPY

I'm sitting on the toilet with my elegant dress bundled up around me when two women walk into the restroom. They don't know I'm here, and I don't bother revealing myself, especially after I hear them mention Matthew's name.

"Who's that woman Matt's with?" one of them asks the other.

"That's his fiancée."

"His fiancée? When did that happen?"

"Just a few weeks ago, I believe."

The woman snorts. "I was just in that bed of his a few months ago. How did he get engaged so fast?"

"No clue. Maybe he was cheating on her," the other suggests. "It wouldn't be the first time you were the other woman," she points out.

He wasn't cheating on me. That was before our arrangement began, but it's not like I can say that.

"Wonder who she is? Or how in the hell she managed to land *him*, of all people. We'd dated and fucked around for years and I never got a proposal." She sounds bitter, angry.

"All I know is that she isn't from around here, and by that, I mean she isn't exactly in our social class. My grandmother is friends with his grandmother. Apparently, there's been a big squabble about his father not wanting him to marry her, but his grandmother really likes her. Matt and his dad haven't talked since . . . well, tonight, I guess."

"So this woman he's with is poor? Like, drives a Prius or some shit?" she jokes.

"Want to know my opinion?"

"Well, I guess I might as well. You're going to tell me anyway."

The other woman snorts. "I think it's all fake. I think she's either using him for his money or he's using her."

"Why in the world would he use her?"

"I don't know. Maybe to get his father off his back? Or maybe there's some kind of clause in his trust fund that states he can't receive the full amount until he's married. Who knows? You know how stuff is done around here. You saw her talking to Jefferson's new wife, didn't you? They were probably exchanging pointers."

So that's what people think? That I'm using him for his money or that he's using me to get money? No one thinks we're just happy and in love? This isn't a world I want to be a part of. But it is his world. If I want him, I have to accept all of him. But can I accept this? These horrible events with even more horrible people?

I stand up and lower my dress back into its original position. I open the door of the stall and step out. The two women gasp as their eyes grow wide with surprise.

I walk up to the sink and wash my hands while they stare blankly at me, watching and waiting to see what I'll say or do. I finish washing my hands and pick up a towel. As I dry my hands, my eyes stay on them. They're still frozen in fear.

"You know," I start, my voice calm, "it's impolite to talk about such private things in public, right?" I wait, but of course, they don't answer. I toss my towel into the basket and take one step closer. They both step back as an automatic response. "Well, I'm sure you two know that. I mean, you are upper-class after all, and that's common knowledge even where I'm from." I look them up and down with a snotty look on my face. "Or . . . are you lower-class like me? I mean, those dresses!" I roll my eyes. "So, whose gold are you two digging?" I lean forward and fake whisper. "Matthew Lewis is mine, so hands off."

One of them, the braver one, stands up tall. "We are not lower-class. We were raised here. We belong here."

"Oh, you could've fooled me. I could've sworn those Louis Vuittons were knockoffs from Maxwell Street Market."

She looks down at her shoes. "These are not knockoffs!"

Clearly, assuming her shoes are knockoffs is way better than actually insulting her. I shrug. "Oh well. Enjoy the party, ladies. And don't forget, check under the stalls before you start gossiping about someone, especially if you have no idea what's really going on. I mean, come on. I'm a gold digger? That's the most creative thing you could come up with? I mean, who knows? Maybe I'm his secret step-sister who's blackmailing him into having an illicit and dirty affair or I'll spill the family secrets." I roll my eyes and shake my head, throwing the restroom door open and strutting out like they were nothing more to me than pesky flies.

But now that I'm out of the restroom, I don't feel as confident. I feel even more like I don't belong. I find Matthew in the middle of a conversation with his father and some other guys. I don't want to interrupt, and honestly, I need a little alone time. I need to think—think about everything we're doing and try to figure out if this is the right decision or not. Am I making a mistake?

Instead of walking back to him, I walk out, needing fresh air in my lungs. I feel trapped in here, like the walls are closing in on me. There's no room to move or breathe. I'm stuck.

The moment I walk outside, I inhale a big gulp of fresh air and feel my head float back down to my body. I'm pretty sure I was moments away from hyperventilating. I need to leave. I need to get out of here. I don't belong—not here with these people. I look for our limo, but there's just a long line of them and I'm not sure which one is ours. Instead of wasting time trying to figure it out, I step up to the street and hail a cab. One stops immediately and I rush to climb in. I quickly rattle off Matthew's address.

When I get to the apartment, I strip out of the dress and leave it lying in the middle of the floor while I pull on my clothes—the clothes that make me feel like myself instead of Cinderella. I think it's time for this story to come to an end. As I start packing, I can't help but think of Cinderella and wonder how she ended up. Sure, the story ends with them married, and then it's "happily ever after." But what if it wasn't? What if the story continued?

Would Cinderella feel out of place when she was by her prince's side? Would he drag her to bizarre parties and expect her to wear ridiculous gowns? Would he insist on her fitting into his world, or would he change to fit into hers? Cinderella was lucky. All she got was a happily ever after. In my mind, that leads the reader to think they lived however the *reader* imagined they'd be happy. But the ending varies depending on who's reading it. They could have children if the reader wants children or already has them. They could end up traveling the world if another reader saw that as a possible future: being in love, kissing, and making love in amazing places whenever they want. But this isn't a storybook. It's my life and there will be a real ending, not just something that's interchangeable.

So what's my ending?

I don't know, but I know I can't see my ending being here by his side, made to feel inferior to him by every watchful eye. I don't want to be forced into ridiculous gowns and parties. I want to be free to live my life the way I see fit, with a man who's in it for the long haul, who's willing to change and grow with me. The more I think about the way he tricked me into this arrangement, the more I realize how wrong it all is. Why was I so willing to just swallow that down and not realize it was him being manipulative—getting his way just like his father?

When I finish packing, I write out a quick note.

. . .

MATTHEW,

I'm sorry for leaving like this, but it's the only way. Please forgive me.

—Poppy

I LEAVE his grandmother's ring on the note and leave both items in the center of my bed. I grab my things and walk out the door for the very last time. I refuse to look back. My choice has been made. I hail another cab and give them my address. I'm going home—back to where I belong, back to where this all started. That seems like a fitting end, right?

TWENTY-EIGHT

MATTHEW

I head over to the women's restroom door and wait. I plan on catching her the moment she steps out so I can drag her out of here. She's better than these people, and now—thanks to her—so am I. Neither of us belongs here anymore. I'm going to tell her I'm sorry for forcing these horrible people on her, and for tricking her into spending time in my fucked-up world. I'll beg until she forgives me.

Two women walk out and I realize one them is an old ex of mine, Trisha.

"Is there anyone else in there?" I ask, grabbing her arm lightly to stop her from walking away.

"No, it was just us two. Your fiancée was in there, but she rushed out after telling us off," she smiles but wipes it away.

"Telling you off? That doesn't sound like her."

She makes a sad face. "Oh, Matthew, don't you realize the people here are lions and you just walked her straight into the den?" Her bright red lips turn up.

I frown. "What was said in there?" I ask, feeling my anger rise.

She shrugs. "Kimberly and I were just trying to figure out how you got engaged so fast since it was only a few months ago that I was the one in your bed. Were you cheating on her?"

I feel the need to vomit all over her ugly-ass dress. "Where is she?"

She rolls her eyes. "I think there's a better question to be asked, don't you?"

I don't know what she's talking about, so I don't reply.

But she steps up to me and places her hands around the back of my neck, locking her fingers together. "Will she stay?" she whispers. "We all know your reputation, Matthew. I wouldn't be surprised if she learned something tonight that she didn't know before she arrived. Something that might have made her change her mind about you."

I reach behind my neck and pull her locked fingers apart. I drop her hands and they fall to her sides. "If you said anything to her . . ." I threaten.

She shrugs carelessly. "I didn't say a word, did I, Kimberly?"

Kimberly steps up. "I can honestly say she didn't say anything." Then she smiles and I know it's not Trisha who said anything. It was her.

I shake my head as I turn on my heel, walking away from them. I quickly sweep the room, realizing she isn't here. She must have left. I walk outside and find the rows of limos. I can't tell which is ours, so I call the driver and he promises to swing around to pick me up. Five minutes later, I'm sliding into the back seat, pushing the button to lower the partition.

"Did you take my fiancée home?" I ask.

"No, sir. I haven't seen her since I dropped you off," he states.

I sink down into the seat, hoping and praying I catch her at home —that she doesn't do anything rash until she talks to me. I can make this right. I *have* to make this right. I can't imagine living my life without her. I refuse to live my life without her.

We finally make it back home and I rush up to the apartment. The place is deathly quiet as I make my way back to her room, which she hasn't been using lately. I walk in and find it empty. I rush to the bathroom, opening the door, but it's empty too. I open the closet door and see that everything is gone. I spin around in a panic and find her ring on top of a single piece of paper. I read over it and my world comes crashing down around me.

I slide the ring into my pocket and crumple the note, tossing it to the side. I grab my phone from my pocket as I head for the door. I call her number again and again on my drive over, but she never answers. Finally, I park in front of her building and rush inside. I try opening her door, but of course, it's locked. I have to settle with pounding on it.

"Poppy, open this door," I demand.

But no sounds come from inside. So I try again. "Poppy, please. We have to talk."

"Go away, Matthew," she finally says.

Just hearing her voice settles my erratic heart rate. I lean my forehead against the door and place my hand next to it as if I could somehow touch her through it. "Please, open up. Let me in, Poppy."

"There's nothing left to say or do. We're over. Give the police the video if you must."

I pull my hand back and hit the door loudly. "Dammit, Poppy! Let me in. I'm not going away. This isn't over. Not for me. Give me a chance to explain."

I hear her unlock it and quickly step back. Moments later, it's swinging open and she's standing before me.

"There's nothing to explain, Matthew." She shakes her head. "It's done. Just leave it."

I rush forward the moment I see her start to close the door. She's in my arms in the next second, and I'm kicking the door closed behind us. "Stop, please. Tell me what happened," I plead.

I have her pinned between me and a wall and I'm not moving until she tells me exactly what happened—what made her run not only from the party, but from me.

"I don't fit in with those people, and that only reminded me that I don't fit into your world. If we get married, I'll just be forced into this little box of expectations—not only by your father, but by your friends too. I don't want that. I don't want to live constantly worrying if I'll be accepted. I don't want the headache of always having to play a role and keep up appearances. That's your world. Not mine."

I shake my head. "That's not my world anymore, and I realized that tonight. I was there waiting by the restroom door for you. I was going to take you away from there. I want you—not them. Not that life."

She shakes her head. "You don't want me. You want the version of me you created: the woman who goes to the gym, who knows which fork to use for the salad, and who wears priceless family heirlooms and doesn't have to bother to shop because the store will come to her. That's not me."

"Dammit, Poppy! I don't care about any of that. You don't want the ring? Fine! I'll give it back to my grandmother. I'll buy you one from Walmart if you want! You don't want the dresses, fine. I'm pretty sure we'll never need another one after we get married anyway. I don't want that world anymore. I want the world we've created. Please . . ." My words fall away as I rest my forehead against hers. "Please, just don't leave. I'll give you anything you want. I'll give up anything you want. I just want you. I only need you."

I take a chance and press my lips to hers. They're stiff—not yet ready to give in. But I breathe her in deeply, letting her scent settle over me like a thick blanket. I can feel her in my mind, heart, and soul. My whole body is consumed with her like she's a drug and I'm addicted. I'm ready to give myself over.

"Please," I beg against her lips. "I only want you. I love you," I say, kissing her jaw and her neck as my hands roam her body, grasping anything I can hold on to.

"Please," I beg again, making my way back to her lips. "I love you," I repeat.

I feel her resolve give way. Her love for me comes rushing out. Her lips move with mine and her hands move up to fist in my hair.

She tugs me closer, even though it's impossible to get any closer without moving through her. Now that she's kissing me, I know that everything will be okay. I pick her up against me and carry her into the living room. I have no idea where her room is, but I don't care. All I need is her. I don't need a bed.

I press her back against the wall again and her hands get busy pulling my clothes away.

"I love you too," she whispers.

I pull back and see fresh tears in her eyes. I raise my hands, wiping them away with my thumbs. "Don't cry. I'm here. We're together. That's all we'll ever need." My lips crash against hers again, and this time, we don't stop. We don't stop kissing, or touching, or loving. One round of lovemaking only leads us to the bedroom where we start all over again.

After round four, we finally fall asleep, holding on to each other like that's the only thing that matters, 'cause it *is* the only thing that matters.

———

IN THE MORNING, I wake and find her sound asleep next to me. She's still naked from the night before, the blanket only covering her lower half as she sleeps on her stomach, facing me. She's beautiful—breathtaking. Why isn't there a stronger word for what she is to me? I'm not just in love with this woman. I am absolutely, completely, irrevocably, totally in love—wrapped up, consumed with her. She's the reason I breathe. She's the reason I was born. She's the reason I'm going to have a good, long, happy life. Gravity isn't holding me here anymore. Only she is.

Her eyes flutter open and lock on mine. A sleepy smile covers her face when she sees me. I lean forward and press a kiss to her head. "Good morning. Did you sleep well?"

She stretches. "Not really. This bed sucks," she laughs out and I join her.

"So, what do you say to going back to my place?"

"It *is* much more comfortable there," she agrees.

"So the wedding is back on?" I say, almost afraid to ask.

"With a few conditions."

I scoot down until we're eye level. "What are your conditions?"

"I never have to go to another fancy party."

"Agreed."

"You won't try forcing me into a round hole when I'm a square peg."

I laugh. "Okay."

"And . . . you wake me up with mind-blowing sex every single morning."

My smile widens. "Oh, I think I can handle those conditions," I agree, rolling us over until I'm hovering above her. "Round five," I say, moving in for a kiss.

TWENTY-NINE

POPPY

"**A**re you ready for our flight, soon-to-be Mrs. Lewis?" he asks, grabbing my hand and pulling me to his chest.

"I'm ready," I agree, moving in to press my lips to his. I've never been more ready to marry this man.

"Good. I might get you to the island and hold you hostage," he jokes, whispering against my lips.

"I wouldn't even fight you."

We land and make it to our little piece of forever. It's exactly the same as I remember it. Nothing has changed except it may be even more beautiful now. The wedding is in three days, and sadly, we're not alone. All the wedding preparations are going into effect. The wedding planner is here with her team of people who boat in every day to get to work, setting up the altar, chairs, and decorations. The chef and his team are here, prepping and preparing for the dinner. And while all this craziness is going on around us, we're not affected by any of it. We stay locked up in our bedroom, feeding each other things we've managed to steal from the kitchen, making love, and sleeping like we haven't gotten to in a decade. Every morning, people boat in only to boat out at night. Nightfall is the only time we have alone, and that's when we emerge from our bedroom, usually to make love in other parts of the house or on the beach, or to cool off in the ocean.

The three days go by in a flash, and if I thought the island was busy before, that was nothing compared with now. Not only is my team here to do my hair and makeup and help me dress, but the guests are coming in too. Matthew's grandmother is the first to arrive, and she looks at the place lovingly, like she hasn't seen it in this lifetime. I help her inside and she sits on the couch.

"How were your travels?" I ask, sitting across from her.

"I don't remember it being quite so long, but maybe that's because nowadays, it's a lot harder for me to sit that long. Or . . . maybe it's because my handsome husband wasn't sitting beside me, distracting me. I haven't been here in almost 15 years. Once he got sick, we stopped coming and I couldn't bear to come here alone."

That breaks my heart. "I bet you have some good memories here, huh?"

She wipes a tear from her eye and nods. "As do you, and plenty more to come, hopefully."

I smile at her sweetness. "I have to go finish getting ready. Will you be okay by yourself?"

"Of course, dear. I know I have some photo albums here somewhere. I'll flip through them. That way, it will feel like Matthew is here with me."

I smile. "Okay. But let me know if you need anything." I stand and walk back into the bedroom to finish my makeup.

I hear boat after boat arriving but don't bother to look out. I'm too focused on getting ready so I can marry the man of my dreams.

The sun begins to set and I know it's finally time. The wedding planner walks into the room and looks down at me. "Everything is perfect. Are you ready?"

I turn away from the mirror. "More than ready."

She hands me my bouquet of wildflowers and opens the door for me.

I walk through the living room to the glass doors that lead to the beach. Peeking out, all the chairs are full. I can see Matthew's best friend and partner, Daniel, and his rock-star fiancée, plus my parents and a few other people I can't place, so I'm sure they're here for Matthew. My guest list was short.

My parents were a little more than shocked when I told them I was engaged to my boss. They'd heard the horror stories about him and the string of expletives that normally followed after I uttered his name. It was like a scene from *Pride and Prejudice* when I explained to them for the fifth time that things had changed and he really was my forever. I left out the bit about me destroying his car and him blackmailing me. We'll save that little gem for another time.

Vivian, my wedding planner, opens the doors and cues the music. Everyone stands as I take my first steps out—barefoot because no one can walk in sand while wearing heels. I feel a little awkward with everyone looking at me, so instead of panicking or looking back at them, I focus on Matthew at the end of the aisle. He's standing there, waiting on me and looking sexy as hell in his khaki pants, bare feet, and white dress shirt, which he's folded up to his elbows. His dark hair is styled neatly and he has a dark shadow growing on his jaw that I wouldn't let him shave. He's smiling his blinding white smile and his dark eyes are watching me intently as I walk closer.

When I get to his side, he almost looks relieved, like he was afraid I'd change my mind and run in the opposite direction. But I'm not running. Not anymore. Not after I've seen the changes he's made to be a better man.

When I stand at his side, he reaches for me, capturing my hands in his, like he's trying to make sure I stay.

"You may be seated," the preacher says to the guests as everyone takes a seat. "We're gathered here today to bring these two people together in holy matrimony. Before we get started, please bow your heads as we pray for the longevity of this blissful union."

He begins to pray, but I can't focus on his prayer. All I can do is look up at Matthew from beneath my lashes with a smile on my face, because he's doing the exact same thing. He isn't paying any more attention to the prayer than I am. He's too busy watching me. In the few minutes this prayer lasts, I see our future flash before my eyes. I see us growing old together. I see the children we'll have—their smiling faces, happy and loved. I see us coming back to this island every year until we're too old to do so. Then I see us drifting away into the unknown, hand in hand. I know it doesn't exactly work like that, but it's a nice vision to have. I've found my best friend—the one who will last a lifetime. I know he'll make me happy and I vow to do the same for him, no matter what it takes.

"Matthew, if you would, present Poppy with her ring and read your vows."

Matthew slides the ring onto my finger, still holding my hand as he looks deeply into my eyes. "Poppy, I'm thankful every single day that I have you. You're the reason my heart beats. You are the air I breathe. You've saved me in more ways than one. You've saved me from dying a bitter old man. The day you walked into my life, I was forever changed. I vow to love you every day for the rest of time. I vow to take care of you, to make you laugh when you're sad, to wipe your tears away, and to always hold you close. I vow myself to you— mind, body, and soul—until I take my last breath."

I feel the tears welling up in my eyes, but I try my hardest to push them back as I slide his wedding band onto his finger. "Matthew, becoming friends with you wasn't easy, but falling in love with you was. It felt like I was standing on the top of a mountain, and every day, I slid down just a little more. And when I fell, you caught me and kept me safe. I vow to do the same for you. I will protect you even when you don't see a threat. I vow to love you with my whole heart, and to work with you every day to keep our marriage strong enough to withstand any storm that comes our way. I vow to stand by your side for the rest of forever."

"By the power vested in me, I now pronounce you and wife. You may kiss your bride," the preacher says, and moments later, I find myself pressed against Matthew's chest, his lips on mine.

I hear the guests as they clap and cheer for us, but it's almost like there's a tunnel between us. It's quiet and everything else is muffled as I stay locked in the world that Matthew and I have created for just the two of us. I kiss him like I won't ever get the chance to kiss him again, feeling every brush of his lips and every sweep of his tongue, burning his scent that's mixed with the smell of salt water into my memory, searing every last detail of this day into my mind.

His hands are on the small of my back, pulling me against him so hard my back arches. My arms are locked around his neck. It's like we're both holding on to one another for dear life, trying to make this moment last a lifetime.

The kiss slows and breaks free. I can feel the heat in my cheeks when my eyes find all the watchful guests, but Matthew still hasn't looked away from me. His eyes are focused on my face as a wide smile of his own takes over.

The music starts up and I go to take a step—to walk back into the house—but he grabs me, picks me up, and cradles me against his chest, walking me back into the house. I lock my hands around the back of his neck and ask, "What's this for?"

"We're married now. I have to carry you over the threshold."

He opens the door with the hand that's under my knees then steps inside. He kicks the door closed behind us with his foot and spins around, both of us falling onto the fluffy white couch, with me still in his arms.

I laugh and giggle from the sudden drop, but he silences me with a kiss. "Thank you for marrying me," he whispers against my lips.

I laugh. "You looked a little nervous out there, like you were worried I might turn and run away."

He smiles. "I was. I thought the ocean wouldn't stop you—you'd swim if you had to," he jokes.

"And where would I go? You're my life now, Matthew. No matter where I run—or swim—I'll always be attached to you. You're my life force."

His dark eyes meet mine and he leans forward, pressing a soft kiss to my jaw. "How long do we have to wait for everyone to leave?"

I laugh. "A while. We still have dinner and cake and speeches. All that fun stuff. Why?"

"I want to rip this dress off of you and make love to you in the ocean."

"Why wait for them to leave? I'd pay to see that show," I joke and he laughs.

"You've already paid by marrying me."

I lean in to feel his lips against mine again, but the wedding planner opens the door. "All right, guys. Everyone's in place. Let's go present the bride and groom."

The two of us untangle ourselves and stand up. Arm in arm, we follow her outside and around the house to where the big white tent is set up. Even from a distance, I can see that everything looks perfect. There are chandeliers hanging in the center with a thousand twinkle lights lighting up the path. There are white tablecloths and beautiful white flower centerpieces. Our guests are already in the tent, standing around the dance floor.

"Let's give a warm welcome to Mr. and Mrs. Matthew Lewis!" the DJ says from his booth, and everyone claps and cheers as Matthew leads me to the center of the dance floor. The music starts up and the sounds of "Can't Help Falling in Love" by Elvis Presley play through the speakers as he spins me around for our first dance.

The festivities go by in a flash. We dance and cut the cake, neither of us shoving it into the other's face. He tosses the garter, and Foster catches it on reflex then quickly tosses it once he realizes what he's done, at which point he throws Matthew an alarmed look. I've never talked to Foster about Bianca, but Matthew's filled me in on their arrangement and I can't help but feel sorry for him. I only hope he can find his own true love and happily ever after someday instead of having it forced on him.

Matthew's boss, Calvin, ultimately ends up with the garter, but he's already married. I toss the bouquet, and to my surprise, Luna, the rock star who's with Daniel, catches it. Her eyes are wide but her lips are turned up in the corners. They're already engaged, so maybe this will help move things forward just a little faster.

Luna walks up to me and pulls me in for a hug. "Thanks, but I've already agreed to walk down the aisle," she jokes.

"Well, maybe now it will happen sooner and I'll be at your wedding."

She shrugs. "We're thinking of eloping. I really like this little island. Can I borrow it?" She laughs.

I shrug. "I don't see why not. It's the perfect honeymoon spot, isn't it?"

She nods. "It's beautiful."

Speeches start up and Matthew's grandmother is the first to move up to the microphone.

"Matthew, Poppy, I can't explain how overjoyed I am that the two of you finally found each other. I have to admit, I was starting to worry about Matthew, but then you walked into his life like it was destiny, and I believe it was. Most people would never notice the change in him, but I've seen every single one and I know you're the key to that. So, as my gift, I would like to sign this island over to you. This place is an island of love that's been in the family for generations. It's only right for it to be passed down to the newest couple. I'm sure it will show you two just as much love as it showed my late husband and me. Enjoy your new home. I love you both."

As she makes her way off the stage, I turn and stare at Matthew with my mouth hanging open. "It's ours?" I ask, full of surprise and excitement.

He nods. "I thought you'd like it."

"Like it? I love it!" I stand up and go to his grandmother as she makes her way back to her seat. I pull her in for a hug and feel more tears burning my eyes.

"Thank you. So much. For everything."

She smiles kindly. "You're welcome, dear. Take care of the place for me."

"You know we will."

I happen to notice my parents walking over and I rush to their sides. "You guys have to meet Matthew." I grab ahold of their arms and force them to walk up to him with me.

"Matthew, I'd like you to meet my parents, Sarah and Jacob. Mom, Dad, this is my new husband, Matthew." I know it's not traditional for my parents to only be meeting my husband on our wedding day, but they live almost a thousand miles away, and we've never been incredibly close—something I hope to work on now.

They shake hands while Mom talks about how beautiful everything is: the island, the wedding, the flower arrangements. Dad threatens Matthew within an inch of his life if he hurts me . . . you know, normal stuff.

As the night draws on, guest start to leave and things begin to get cleaned up. The wedding is officially over, but our marriage is just beginning.

THIRTY

MATTHEW

The guests leave and the party team cleans up a little before heading out. They'll tear down the tent, tables, and chairs tomorrow when the sun is out. Now that we're alone on the island again, I pull her over to the shore. I spin her around and start lowering her zipper and unbuttoning her dress. It falls down around her feet in the sand and she turns to face me, wearing nothing but a light blue thong. She lifts her arms and starts taking the pins out of her hair while I unbutton my shirt and free myself from my clothing. Naked and hand in hand, we walk into the water.

I lead her in deep, until the water is touching our shoulders, and I pick her up against me, looking into her midnight eyes as the big moon shines back in her pupils. "You're breathtaking," I breathe out, and she smiles.

Her cheeks, even in the soft light of the moon, are glowing pink. I can't help but run the backs of my fingers across them. I move in slowly for a kiss—a kiss that quickly becomes rushed and urgent. I feel my body coming to life and know it's never felt this way before her.

People ask: *How do you know if you've found the one you're meant to spend your life with?* And this is it. Everything is different. Kisses are more intense. Words spoken between us are more than just words. They can be lethal—sharp as the world's strongest blade—but they can also heal as they take all that pain away and leave no scar. A simple touch isn't just a brush of a hand. It feels like there's power in that touch that makes your hair stand on end and your body tingle like it's coming alive in a whole new way. If you don't know if the person you're with is the one, then they're not the one. From the moment I met her, deep down, I knew she was the one. It's always and has only ever been her.

Her hand moves up, her fingers threading into my hair as she tugs at it, breaking our kiss. "Take me to bed, Matthew."

Still holding her body against me, I turn and walk out of the water, then into the house, with water dripping off our bodies. I carry her into the bedroom and kick the door closed between us. Then we both fall into bed, the blankets sticking to our wet bodies. But neither of us cares about the bed. All that matters is that we're together from now until the end of our days. And I know that even that won't stop us. Wherever I go, heaven or hell, I'll be waiting with open arms for her to come running into them after taking her last breath. Love isn't just an earthly feeling. It's eternal. It will follow me to the heights of heaven or the depths of hell—always perfect, whole, unscathed.

I push into her and she welcomes me with fire, but it doesn't burn and it isn't painful. No, this is the heat—the passion—of our love. It's as hot as molten lava and as real as anything you can reach out and touch. These aren't just chemicals in our brains. It's not just some emotion we can't see, feel, or taste. Our love soaks into all of our senses. It makes touching one another feel heavenly. It makes the flavor of our wedding cake sweeter. And as I push into her, the sounds of our love fill the room.

———

OUR WEEK in paradise goes by in a perfect flash. How I wish we could stay locked up here forever. As I pack our things into the boat, she stands back, looking over the place like she's leaving her heart behind.

"We'll come back," I promise her.

"I know." She smiles. "Every time we have to go, it just gets harder to leave this piece of perfection behind."

"Well, it's ours now. Are there any changes you want to make? Expand, paint, remodel?"

Her head whips around to stare me down as she frowns. "No way. This place is classic and timeless. It's like it's locked away, guarded from time and change. It's perfect."

I smile at her words. "All right, everything is packed up. You ready to hit the water?"

"No," she says, dragging her feet on the way to the dock, making me laugh.

"I have another surprise for you."

She smiles now. "You do?"

"Mm-hmm."

"Tell me!"

I laugh as I pick her up against me and set her in the boat. "No way. What fun would that be? It's a surprise."

She frowns as she sits down and crosses her arms over her chest. "I hate surprises."

"No, you don't," I argue.

"Well, this time I do."

"You really want to know?"

Her arms uncross now and she sits up, giving me her blinding smile as she nods.

I pull out my phone and pull up the pictures of the house I purchased. I turn it around so she can see the screen. "I bought us a new house, just outside the city."

Her mouth drops open and her eyes widen. "You did?"

I shrug as I flip through the pictures for her. "I thought it would be nice to have a place that's just ours—a brand-new home where we can build our story. You know, in case we want children or land. We'll have a master suite with a walk-in closet, and a bathroom with a jacuzzi tub. There are three more bedrooms for future children, or we can turn them into other things. No matter what we want in life, we'll have the room for it."

She smiles wide and throws herself into my lap, giggling and kissing me. I'm lost in her, and any thought of leaving doesn't even register as I hold her against me.

"So you like it?" I ask around our kiss.

She smiles and nods, but doesn't stop kissing me.

"It's perfect," she says, pulling back to look me in the eye.

"Stop that," I say, voice hard.

"Stop what?"

"Stop trying to distract me with your midnight eyes. We have to leave. We have a flight to catch." I can't hold back my smile.

She laughs. "But I just realized that we've never done it on the boat."

She's right. "All right," I agree, lifting my hips and pushing my shorts down as she moves to straddle me.

With one arm wrapped around her lower back and the other between her shoulder blades, I pull her down on me and enter her like home. The plane can wait, and if it doesn't, there are other options. But being with her in this way will always be the most important thing. She'll always come before everything else—always top priority.

With the light breeze blowing and the boat softly rocking, we both come undone in record time. I fill her with every last drop and she tenses around me, welcoming it like it quenches a thirst. I kiss her one last time, knowing that this is how we'll always be. I'll make sure of it—never slacking on my efforts to keep her happy. Never pushing her to the back burner for something more pressing. She is my life.

When we've both managed to regain control of our bodies, she removes herself from me to fix her clothing, then she takes her seat with a smile and I start up the boat. As we make our journey across the water, I can't help but take her in: her wide smile, her shining eyes, her dark hair blowing in the breeze, the way her skin shimmers when the light hits it, and her sun-kissed shoulders. I burn it all into my memory, knowing that each year we come here, we'll both be a little different—a little older, but still just as much in love.

I used to worry about where the future would lead me, but with her by my side, I no longer worry, because I know it doesn't matter. It doesn't matter if I lose all my money or all my possessions, because I'll always have her. And as long as I always have her, I'll always be rich.

Finding that one person who was meant for you—finding true love—is more important than anything money could ever buy. And if you have your other half, hold on to them. Don't let the pressures of the world get you down or tear you apart. We're born alone and we die alone, but we don't have to *be* alone. As long as you've loved, you'll always have that person with you, even in the darkest of times . . . even in the end.

She looks over at me and although it's too loud to hear with the wind in our ears, she mouths, "I love you."

I smile. "I love you. Forever."

If you LOVED *Breaking up with My Boss* then make sure you check out Foster and Harley's story in *My Accidental Forever!*

MY ACCIDENTAL FOREVER
SNEAK PEEK

First he bailed me out of jail.
Then we ended up accidentally married...yeah I know,
it's a wild ride.
Thats when I found out he was already promised to
someone else.
Cue operation secretly getting divorced and pretending
I'm not falling for him...

CHAPTER ONE

HARLEY

"I'm engaged!" my best friend, Cora, nearly screams as she jumps up and down in front of me. Her right hand is fanning her face. The left is held out, showing off her beautiful, sparkling diamond ring for me to see.

I do my best to force a smile, hoping and praying that it looks genuine, but who am I kidding? I'm not good at faking anything. My resting bitch face always gives me away. "Congratulations," I say with as much enthusiasm as I can muster as I take her left hand in mine and look at her ring.

She pulls me forward into a rib-crushing hug. Her giggles turn to tears. "Oh, Harley. I didn't think this day would ever come," she says, sniffling. "Now you're the only one that's left."

Yeah, rub it in. That makes things better.

Let me start by saying that I'm not your *stereotypical* girl. I've never been one to dream of my prince charming or the perfect wedding. It's not that I'm just dying to get married, but it sucks that I'm the last of my friends who is still single. Sarah has two kids already. Jessica is pregnant. Lilly, Meredith, and now Cora are all engaged. And myself...well, I have a couple of foster dogs at home, no real boyfriend, and no intentions of settling down any time soon. I feel like everyone is just way better at this adulting stuff than I am. It feels like I just discovered that I'm in a race and I'm already in last place.

"I know," I agree. "But I think I'll always be the single one. You know, the cool aunt who keeps the secrets and sneaks alcohol at all the kid parties," I joke, and she pretends to ignore the hint of sadness in my tone.

She forces a laugh and playfully smacks my arm. "You're a riot," she says, blowing me off. "Seriously, aren't there any guys who may stick? I know you're seeing like three dudes right now right?"

I roll my eyes. "I am not *'seeing'* three of them," I argue.

She gasps. "You are too! There's Brett, the motorcycle racer. There's Tony, the almost MMA fighter. And there's Will, the aspiring musician. You don't think any of them will stick?" She sits back down in the chair across from my desk and I follow suit.

"Well, let's see. Brett," I start ticking them off on my fingers, "he's already out of the picture. He's gone to Florida for a race. We went one two dates and no I didn't sleep with him." I hold up my second finger. "Tony, he stopped talking to me when I didn't put out on the first date," I say, and she gasps as she leans forward to smack me across the arm. I quickly dodge away, out of her reach. "And Will, he's still around but it's nothing serious."

She shakes her head. "How could you leave Tony like that? He was hot as hell, Harley!"

I nod. "I know, but he seriously sucked at fighting and thought he was amazing and I'm not down with a dude that expects me to suck his dick because he bought me a steak. Fuck right off bro." I shrug. "I want a winner, not a loser who always has black eyes," I joke.

She rolls her blue eyes and shakes her head, making her red curls sway with the motion. "Seriously, you keep being this picky and you will end up alone."

I laugh. "Well, I'm always going to be this picky, but while you guys are all tied down to your husbands and kids and PTA meetings,

I'll be out living my best life and traveling the world. So, who's really losing here?" I ask with a wink, but keep my tone light and playful as a smile stretches across my face. We both know I'm kidding but what she doesn't see is how much I'd actually love to be *tied down* like that.

She giggles. "I guess it all depends on what you want. I want to be married, have a couple of kids, always have my best friend with me, through thick and thin. But good for you for not following along with all these boring traditions." She rolls her eyes and I can tell she doesn't believe a word of my story.

"Yeah, I mean, all that marriage stuff is good for you and the girls, but I'm just not that type."

"That won't stop you from joining us at the bar tonight, right? To celebrate?" She offers up a smile as her shoulder rise.

"I wouldn't miss it," I promise. "I'm so happy for you babe. Just because I might not want the same things as you doesn't ever diminish my happiness for you and all our friends."

"Good," she says, standing up and heading for the door to my office. "I'll text you the details, but plan for a wild night," she says, pointing at me.

I hold up my hand and wave as she makes her way out of my office. The door softly clicks closed behind her and I'm finally alone. A long breath leaves my lips slowly as I lean my head back against my chair. My eyes find the white ceiling and flutter closed.

Like I said, I don't want marriage. I don't want to be tied down. I don't want to go to sleep with the same man every night. At this point, I'm not sure if I'm reminding myself of this or trying to convince myself. Jealously and guilt naw at my stomach. I hate that I feel this way. I don't want to be jealous and that's why I feel guilty. My jealously got in the way of being happy for Cora, and she deserves nothing less. Tonight, I will be happy for her. I will be excited, even though it feels like all my friends are growing up faster than I am. They're moving on with their kids, husbands, and fiancés and here I am, scraping together my pennies for the fifty cent drafts at Stella's. My life has seriously gone off the rails.

With that thought, I think I'll take off early today. I close all the windows that are open on my computer and shut it down. I shut off the lamp on my desk, grab my phone, keys, and bag and start for the door. I lock my office behind me and then make my way through the shelter. The sound of barking fills my ears as I make my way down the hallway and into the front lobby. Jenna is standing behind the desk, her attention on the computer screen. When she hears my footsteps, she looks up. "Taking off early today?"

"Yep, I've just had all the fun I can handle," I tell her, leaning against the counter with my keys and phone in each hand.

"Any plans? Got a hot date or anything for the weekend?"

I roll my eyes. "No hot date, not yet anyway. My friend just got engaged so we're going out to celebrate. Fingers crossed I find a hottie there."

She giggles and I wink. "See ya Monday."

"Enjoy your weekend, and try not to catch any diseases this weekend," she jokes.

I laugh. "Same to you, my friend. Same to you." I push my way out of the swinging doors and head for my car in the parking lot.

I open the door to my blacked out Jeep Wrangler and climb behind the wheel. I drop my bag into the passenger seat and drop my keys into the cup holder as my foot presses the break and my finger finds the start button. The motor turns over and purrs to life. The air that blows out of the vents is hot from sitting around all day so I roll down the windows until it cools off. Summer is just starting and already it's unbearable.

I click my seatbelt and shift into drive. Looking both ways, I pull out onto the nearly empty street. As I drive, I can't help but to feel more alone than usual. Maybe it's because my only single friend is now on the marriage train. Her and the girls will be doing married lady things and I'll be forever alone and left out. On the sidewalk across the street, a man and a woman walk hand in hand. He looks at her and she looks back with a smile. He tugs her to him and they kiss.

I roll my eyes and scoff. "Oh come on! Get a room," I mumble to myself.

I guess I should get it all out of my system now. I have to be happy and excited for Cora. I can't let my bitterness and jealously ruin this for her or me. This could be one of the last nights we get to party together. Soon, she'll be consumed with wedding planning and then married life. Maybe it's time I find a few unmarried women to kick it with.

Fuck that. I need to stop thinking about marriage altogether. I'm twenty-four. I have a full-time job making very little money. In fact, more than half my income goes to paying my car and bills. Luckily for me, I don't eat much. And I date a lot so I get free meals, but still. Does that scream ready for marriage and kids to you? It doesn't to me. I need to grow up before I can think of settling down with anyone. I need to be more responsible before I think of having kids. Or...do I even want kids? Maybe I can find a man like me, always ready to have fun and doesn't want to be tied down. Now, that would be the life. But I'm sure my girlfriends would disagree.

I pull into the driveway and park my Jeep. I shut the engine off and grab my things as I unbuckle. I hop out and before I get to the door, I can hear the dogs barking with excitement from inside. They're my kids, for now anyway.

I unlock the door and let myself in. Four dogs greet me and I fall to my knees to play with them in the doorway.

Bob licks my face. Gizmo is jumping all around, wagging his tail and beating me to death with it. Juno is hanging out in the back, she's the newest addition and isn't sure what's going on yet. And Dozer, well he's all over me, making me fall back until I'm laying on my back on the floor. I can't hold back my giggles at how excited they are.

"Okay, okay. Who wants to go outside?" I ask, pushing them back as I work to get myself off the floor. They all start barking, whining, and running for the back door. I walk through the living room, kitchen, and into the laundry room where the back door is located. I unlock it and open it, and all the dogs go running out at full speed. I step outside to watch them run and play in the fenced in back yard. I got lucky with this place.

This is my grandmother's house and I only got it after she moved into her assisted living condo across town. The place is paid for, but I still have to pay water, power, and property taxes. Plus the upkeep of fixing anything that breaks and paying the company that mows the lawn. It's a great place and I couldn't even find an apartment on what I make, especially one that is okay with me having foster dogs. But fostering the animals is a part of my job, and it's often one of my favorite parts.

I work as the PR director for a local no shelter so I handle all the advertising, adoption and foster events. But *no kill* also means non-profit. I get paid very little. I know I could probably go elsewhere with my talents, but this is where my heart is. My dad once said, *find a job you love and you'll never work a day in your life.* Well, I may have taken that a little too seriously. There should have been something in that speech that included money somewhere, you know, so I can provide for myself a little better. Don't get me wrong, I make enough to stay afloat, but it would be nice to not constantly be trying to figure out if I can afford to go on a three day weekend once a year or get my eyebrows done. It would be nice just to skip out of work for a fancy lunch and a shopping spree, but this is the life I chose. Sometimes, I think I'm doing this whole adulting thing wrong.

As I watch the dogs run and play, my phone chimes from my back pocket. I pull it free and read the message on the screen from Cora.

Stella's Bar, eight o'clock. Be prepared to party it up!

I laugh and shake my head before turning the screen off and sliding it back into my pocket. I stretch and let out a loud yawn. Maybe I just didn't get enough sleep last night. Maybe I'll take a nap before hitting the town. That's probably why I feel weird today; it's not because Cora is engaged. That thought makes me feel a little bit better.

I clap my hands and call for the dogs. They come running immediately and we all go back inside. They rush off to the living room, ready to lay down, a couple playing tug-of-war with their rope toy while I make myself a late lunch. I eat a sandwich and some chips and drink a glass of tea before locking the house and going to the bedroom for a nap. I leave the bedroom door open and every single dog climbs into bed with me. I really need a bigger bed.

The alarm on my phone goes off two hours later and my eyes flutter open. I silence the alarm and look toward the window where the late afternoon sun is filtering through the blinds. The dust particles in the air are light up like glitter as they float down to the ground. It's five o'clock, but thanks to it being early summer, the sun is still high in the sky, not ready to go down and call it a day yet.

I stretch and yawn, trying to force myself to wake up. Finally, I push myself to my feet and trudge to the shower. I strip out of my jeans and *don't buy, adopt* T-shirt I wore to work today. I climb beneath the hot flow of water and tilt my head back, allowing the hot water to wash over my hair and face.

I take extra time in the shower since there is still a couple of hours until the party. I shave and wash and condition my hair. I do a hair mask and a face mask, and then use my in-shower lotion so I'm nice and soft. Finally, I have nothing left to do so I climb out and wrap a towel around myself.

I decide to throw on some pajamas while I do my hair and makeup and find something for dinner. I end up eating a salad on the couch while my hair air dries. Once I finish, I'm back in the bathroom to get ready for the long night of partying that's sure to come.

At seven I'm finally fully dressed and ready to have a night out on the town. I stand back and look myself over in the mirror. My black skinny jeans hug every curve of my hips and thighs. The holes and rips from the distressing gives a peek at my tanned legs. I tuck in a simple white tank and throw on a black and gold belt. I pair the outfit with a pair of black high heeled boots. I went extra heavy on the eye makeup, with a smoky eye, false lashes, and a shiny lip. My long dark hair is full of curls and body, looking a little messy just like I like it. I grab my purse and head for the car, more than ready to celebrate with my girls.

I walk into Stella's and the place is already crowded. Every table is occupied. Every barstool already taken. The dance floor is filled with moving bodies and groups stand in almost every free area of the bar. I find the girls in a back corner booth. I put a smile on my face and make my way back.

"Harley!" Cora yells with a smile when she sees me. She rushes up to me, throwing her arms around my neck for a big hug.

I giggle. "You hit the sauce already?," I ask her, hugging her back and picking pink boa feathers out of my mouth.

She pulls back and laughs, smoothing down her boa. "I might have pregamed," she winks at me dramatically. "You ok? You seemed a little sad today."

I wave her off. "I was just tired...and hungry. Both problems have been solved now. I'm good. Now, what do you say to getting hammered and not remembering this night?" I ask with a wide smile.

She throws her arms in the air and lets out a long howl before leading me the rest of the way to the table where shots are already lined up.

Shots are poured quickly and the beer seems to be in an endless supply. I don't remember making the conscious decision to attempt to kill myself with alcohol tonight, but that's apparently what I've done. My vision is blurring and my body feels extra sensitive. Of course, that could have something to do with the arms I'm engulfed in. A sexy man who's tall, muscular, has thick dark hair, and a scruff to his jaw is holding me close, his body grinding against mine.

"What's your name?" I ask over my shoulder as I wiggle my ass against him.

His hands tighten on my hips. " Foster," he whispers low in my ear. "What's yours?"

I turn around and wrap my arms around his neck. With a smile I say, "Harley."

"Harley, huh? Don't think I've heard that outside of the Joker cartoon."

I laugh. "Yeah, I get that a lot. I'm not named after Harley Quinn. My daddy was a biker." I shrug one shoulder and play indifferent.

He leans in closer and his hot breath washes over my dry lips. "What do you say to coming home with me tonight?" His lips press against my jaw and it makes my eyes flutter closed.

"I would love to, but I'm here with some friends, celebrating an engagement."

"Not yours, I hope." There's a hint of a smile on his lips and his brow arches as he awaits my answer.

I laugh. "No, never mine. I'm still too wild to get married. I like to have too much fun." I give him a teasing smile.

"Is that so?" he asks, slowly leaning in to test the waters. I know what he wants and the alcohol in my system makes me lean forward, capturing his lips with my own. His lips are soft and teasing. They move slowly at first but then pick up speed and intensity. They part and his tongue makes its way into my mouth. He tastes of beer and spiced rum and his scratchy beard feels good against my soft skin.

His hands are big and strong, but soft, telling me that he probably has some kind of corporate office type job. We're both in the same boat tonight, just looking to blow off some steam and maybe get laid. But who am I to judge? I want him just as much as he seems to want me. His hands travel my body, squeezing my hips, rubbing up and down my back, and back down again to grasp my hips. His lips fall from mine, kissing across my jaw and to my neck. I want nothing more than to go back to his place and fall into his bed, where he can show me how good he is with the rest of his body, but I'm here for Cora, I remind myself.

"Let's get another shot," I tell him, pulling back but keeping his hand in mine while I drag him over to the bar.

He stands at my side. "Are you sure you can't sneak away from them for the night?"

I smile. "I probably could, but I won't. Tonight isn't about me," I say, but I'm not sure if I'm telling him or reminding myself. I seem to be doing a lot of that tonight.

"And I can't talk you into changing your mind?"

I shake my head. "Not tonight," I say around a teasing smile.

He pulls his wallet out of his back pocket and hands over a card. "Well, call me when you do."

I look at the card and see his name Foster Wilder, Wilder Industries. And his cell phone number. Since we've been dancing, I don't have my purse with me so I slide the card down into my bra for safe keeping. "I will call you some time," I promise.

"I hope so," he says, leaning in toward me. He smells delicious, like deep oak, a hint of sunshine and summer breeze. He smells clean and fresh, but also thick and woodsy at the same time. It's the perfect combination to have my mind spinning.

"So, tell me about yourself, Foster," I say, sliding my money over for a drink.

He smiles and it makes my breath hitch in my throat. "Well, after college I went to work at the family business. Since then, I've been climbing my way up the ladder. Hopefully earn those CEO letters behind my name someday."

"How old are you?" I'm handed my drink and I stir it before taking a sip.

"Thirty-two," he answers. "How old are you?"

"Twenty-four, but I don't have some fancy corporate job. I work as the PR director at a local no-kill shelter."

He nods and the corners of his mouth turn up into a smile. "So, you like animals?"

"I love animals. What's not to love? I handle all the companies advertising and I plan all the adoption benefits we hold. I also foster dogs."

His brow raises like he's impressed. "How charitable of you. What do you like to do when you're not working?"

I shrug. "I'm a free spirit. I like to do anything as long as it's fun.

I'm a play it by ear kind of person. I never make plans. I always just... do whatever I want."

He smiles. "Seems like we have a lot in common." He leans forward and I feel the air between us growing thick. Slowly, we both lean inward and I can't wait to feel his lips against mine again.

"Harley! Get your butt over here!" one of the girls yell, and it steals my attention. I look over my shoulder at them, laughing, talking, dancing, and having fun. I turn my attention back to Foster. "I guess I should be getting back, but I got your number."

"You better use it too," he says around a flirty smile.

"I will," I promise, a shy smile of my own breaking through as I turn and walk away from him. I take my place back with the girls and they're all giddy about my recent interaction with the sexy guy. I dodge the million questions they throw at me as I look over my shoulder and throw him one last glance.

**

I don't know what happens, but once I pulled myself away from Foster, the drinks seemed to hit harder. I'm barely able to stay on my feet as we all dance. I open my eyes and look around, wondering how exactly I ended up on the top of the table without realizing it.

"Ma'am, you have to get down. Come on," the security guard says, reaching up for me.

"What? Go away," I start, but his hand catches my wrist and he pulls me downward. I fall and he catches me in his arms, but the table I was standing on topple and falls to its side, clanging loudly off the floor.

"That's it. You've had enough. Time to go," he says, setting me on my feet and pulling me toward the doors.

"Wait. What?" I ask, looking around for someone to help but he's pulling me out too quickly. My vision is too blurred to make out any of my friends. The next thing I know, we're outside and the air is cool. I breathe it in deeply as I turn to face him.

"You need a cab or something?"

I frown. "No, I can get my own cab," I insist. "Why am I being thrown out? My friends are still in there, looking for me."

He crosses his arms over his big chest and shakes his head. "You know you're not allowed to dance on the tables. This is a bar, not a strip club."

I gasp. "Screw you, guy!" I poke him in the chest with my index finger as I try to step around him, but he matches me step for step. "I'm just going to go inside the moment you stop watching," I say, holding my hands into fists at my sides.

He rolls his eyes. "Yeah, like this is my first encounter with a drunk girl. I'm going to be standing right inside that door. Try coming in again and I'll call the police. We have them on speed dial here. Don't try me. Just go home and sleep it off." Without another word, he spins around and walks back into the bar.

I take a deep breath and try to cool myself down. What a bunch of shit. I wasn't doing anything wrong. So what if I danced on a table? It's not like I killed someone. It's not like anyone was hurt.

With a surge of bravery and the feeling of being mistreated, I head back into the bar. I walk right through the doors and in several steps, but then someone catches me around my waist and drags me back out.

"I told you," he says in my ear. "You didn't even wait a whole minute!" He has a hint of amusement in his voice but I don't find this funny.

"Let me go!" I order. "Get your hands off me." I fight against his hold.

Finally he sets me back down on the sidewalk outside of the bar. I spin around to face him. "What's your problem? It's not like you're the king of the bar. I wasn't hurting anyone."

"That's not the point. Our insurance doesn't cover drunk girls dancing on tables. If you fell off and broke your neck and tried to sue, you'd shut us down."

I nearly snort. "Oh, I wouldn't fall and if I did, I wouldn't sue. It's my dumb decision to dance on the table."

"Exactly, dumb decision. Now, go home and sleep it off."

"You sleep it off," I argue.

"Is there a problem here?" a man says and I turn to look at him. It's a police officer.

"No, there's no problem. Is there?" I look at the security guard.

"Actually, I've had to remove this woman from the bar twice now."

"Ma'am," the police officer says. "I suggest you take the kind hint this man is giving you and take yourself home before I have to arrest you."

My eyes grow wide. "Arrest me for what?" I ask, shocked.

"Drunken disorderly conduct," he answers.

The security guard goes back inside, leaving me alone with the officer. "Look, my friends are still in there. She's just gotten engaged and we're supposed to be celebrating. Can I please just go back in? I promise I'll behave." I offer him up a smile and bat my lashes a little.

"I'm sorry, ma'am, but I can't allow that."

"Not even if I show you my—?" My hands are already on the bottom of my top, lifting it upward.

"That's it," he says, cutting me off. His hands catch my wrists and he somehow manages to spin me around so that they're behind my back. The next thing I know, I'm in a pair of handcuffs and being shoved into the back of the police car.

Fuck. I really did it this time.

Read the rest of *My Accidental Forever*

READ THE REST OF THE LOVE YOU FOREVER SERIES

The Wrong Brother

Marrying My Best Friend's BFF

Rocking His Fake World

My Accidental Forever

The F It List

ALSO BY ALEXIS WINTER

Slade Brothers Series

Billionaire's Unexpected Bride

Off Limits Daddy

Baby Secret

Loves Me NOT

Best Friend's Sister

Grand Lake Colorado Series

A Complete Small-Town Contemporary Romance Collection

Castille Hotel Series

Hate That I Love You

Business & Pleasure

Baby Mistake

Fake It

South Side Boys Series

Bad Boy Protector-Book 1

Fake Boyfriend-Book 2

Brother-in-law's Baby-Book 3

Bad Boy's Baby-Book 4

Mountain Ridge Series

Just Friends: Mountain Ridge Book 1

Protect Me: Mountain Ridge Book 2

Baby Shock: Mountain Ridge Book 3

Make Her Mine Series

My Best Friend's Brother

Billionaire With Benefits

My Boss's Sister

My Best Friend's Ex

Best Friend's Baby

ALL BOOKS CAN BE READ AS STAND-ALONE READS WITHIN THESE SERIES

ABOUT THE AUTHOR

Alexis Winter is a contemporary romance author who loves to share her steamy stories with the world. She specializes in billionaires, alpha males and the women they love.

If you love to curl up with a good romance book you will certainly enjoy her work. Whether it's a story about an innocent young woman learning about the world or a sassy and fierce heroine who knows what she wants you're sure to enjoy the happily ever afters she provides.

When Alexis isn't writing away furiously, you can find her exploring the Rocky Mountains, traveling, enjoying a glass of wine or petting a cat.

You can find her books on Amazon or at https://www.alexiswinterauthor.com/

Follow Alexis Winter below for access to advanced copies of upcoming releases, fun giveaways and exclusive deals!

Made in the USA
Las Vegas, NV
11 February 2021

17621285R00125